I0570551

Union of the Snake

KC Burn

Copyright © 2015 by KC Burn
All rights reserved.
No part of this book may be reproduced in any form or by any electronic or
mechanical means, including information storage and retrieval systems, without
written permission from the author, except for the use of brief quotations in a
book review.
This is a work of fiction. Names, characters, places, and incidents either are the
products of the author's imagination or are used fictitiously. Any resemblance to
actual persons, living or dead, businesses, companies, events, or locales is entirely
coincidental.
1st Edition: 2015 in the Come Undone anthology
2nd Edition: 2016
Editor: Tamara Eaton
Cover Art: Winterheart Design (www.winterheart.com)

ISBN-13: 978-0-9981807-4-8

DEDICATION

For the love of guyliner.

ACKNOWLEDGMENTS

Thanks to Louisa and Sabrina for inviting me to write this story. I'd been having a hard time getting into the mental headspace for writing after some family issues, and having this goal allowed me to find my way back..

CHAPTER ONE

"Get in there, you human scum. Your first fight is tomorrow."

The larger prison guard slammed the base of his lance into Zerek's shoulder blade, sending him stumbling into a cell. He caught himself, barely, before slamming his head against one of the rough, uneven rocks that formed the walls of the tiny enclosure.

The Hilruda guards had done nothing to loosen the bonds, which held Zerek's wrists during his sentencing. With a bit of determination and strength, he should be able to use those damp, lichen-covered rocks to work his way free. Otherwise, he'd be fighting the next day with a fairly severe handicap. More severe than the concussion making his vision blur.

Motherless, cheating, sons of oxen humpers.

Once the guards left, the only light left was the dim orange flicker of torchlight. Barely enough to see his hands in front of his face, but he'd heard enough stories about the Stony Gate prison facility to know the comfort and well being of the inmates were immaterial. Especially the human ones.

His twin life goals had been to both avoid ending up in Stony Gate and to be prepared in case he did. Fortunately, he'd failed at only one of those goals, so he was confident he had a decent chance of surviving the pit fights until he could figure a way out of this cesspool. Escapes weren't unheard of, but they were quite rare. Zerek intended to become the feature of whispered stories told around the work camps. Well, he already was. He had a reputation to live up to, and it didn't include engaging in prisoner exploitation combat to gratify the increasingly rapacious appetite of the Hilruda.

Forgoing the ratty and likely parasite-ridden bed for now, he settled on the chilly floor by the most lethal outcropping of stone and began the laborious process of cutting through his bonds.

1

Soon, he fell into an almost hypnotic rhythm, the rasp of rope on rock giving him something to focus on besides the echoing sounds of human suffering. He'd never heard how many people Stony Gate could hold, but what did numbers matter? Humans had been ground down to little more than slaves of the Hilruda over the past couple of generations. No one could take the Hilruda to task for their ill treatment of any human, never mind overcrowding in a facility filled with people deemed criminals. Even if most of them were innocent.

"Hey, newbie." The whispered words startled him enough that he allowed a momentary pause in his work, but staying calm and being able to assess new information as quickly as possible were key ingredients to surviving to his ripe old age of twenty-nine.

"Yes?" Zerek wasn't about to get friendly. Not until he had a better idea of what he'd be facing.

"Whatcha in for?"

"Smuggling." Most people in here were innocent. He wasn't one of those people, but his life's work fell on the right side of his own moral compass, so he didn't feel a smidgeon of guilt about breaking any of the Hilruda laws imposed since the Bitter Silence. Neither was he in here to make friends. If he could, he'd free everyone, but those were lofty goals for another day, another life. He had to get himself out of here first.

"Smuggling? I heard the masters say they'd arrested a whole crew of smugglers, including Zerek himself."

Zerek's teeth clenched and he put more effort into separating the rope between his wrists. With the Hilruda—no way would he call them masters—advertising his capture from one end of the planet to the other, restoring his reputation was going to prove difficult. But not impossible, especially if he escaped Stony Gate unscathed.

"A whole crew?" If that toad loving son of a goat who'd betrayed him managed to get his entire crew captured, Zerek's first stop would be to Gress's misbegotten hovel where he'd strip his skin to make new boots.

"Oh, yes. Some of the guards were practically giggling, they were so happy." The disembodied voice coughed. "Uh, I guess you knew them."

Zerek shrugged, even though it was likely his new friend couldn't see. The guards that had brought him down from his sentencing hadn't giggled. He wasn't even sure they knew how to laugh, but then, most Hilruda looked like they'd swallowed their own teeth. "Dunno. I don't even know if Zerek's real. Must be propaganda." Despite the fact he was involved in a lot of illegal operations, Zerek was well aware the story of his exploits gave people a small sliver of hope and made the Hilruda rabid. His capture alone was a huge victory for the Hilruda. Even the rumor of his crew's capture would grind the spirit of his fellow humans into the mud.

"Zerek exists. I know a guy who did business with another guy who sold him something."

He bit his lip against a rueful chuckle. He much preferred that sort of ephemeral "proof" of his existence. But another guy who sold him something had also sold him out to the fucking Hilruda. When he got out of here—and rescued his crew, if their capture wasn't just propaganda—he was going to have to revisit his entire network and reassess them.

A hacking cough lasting for several painful seconds prevented his companion from speaking, and when the episode was over, ragged breathing followed.

The damp, chill, and lichen spawned illnesses and prevented healing. He doubted many of the inmates received medical care. They'd be lucky if they received full rations of food and water.

Zerek concentrated on his bonds again, ignoring the sting of raw flesh on his wrists. After a few more minutes of intense exertion, the rope parted. With some effort, he held in a shout of triumph. Bringing attention to himself was the last thing he wanted.

Now that his arms were free, he noticed the knotted muscles in his shoulders and the ache in his neck. He'd been bound for almost a day—his capture and sentencing had been alarmingly swift, and he thanked his lucky stars that they hadn't bound his hands behind his back. Otherwise, he'd be in much worse shape for a fight tomorrow.

Stretching, he sifted through what he knew about the pit fights. Almost all of it hearsay, as he'd never been able to track down any of the people who'd supposedly escaped, assuming they were still alive somewhere.

Zerek listened carefully, but couldn't hear the murmur of voices, or nearby sounds of any other inmates aside from the still labored breathing of the guy who'd spoken to him.

"Hey, you still there?" Maybe he shouldn't have been so dismissive of his companion. There was no point in asking if he was okay. Anyone in here wasn't okay, and what was he going to do if the guy needed help? Call a healer? Be like trying to capture the wind.

"Yes." The voice was weak, and Zerek steeled himself against caring. If he had the wherewithal to rescue every damned person in the building, then burn this cesspit to the ground, he would.

"You been in the pit? Got any tips?"

"Yeah. Don't lose."

The guard's three fingers bit into Zerek's bicep as the fucker helpfully "guided" Zerek through the winding tunnels of Stony Gate. He'd been rousted from his cell as unceremoniously as he'd been locked in. Although neither of the guards said anything, it was obvious the time for his fight had come.

He took careful note of the path and landmarks, but nothing struck him as an escape route. The couple of passageways they passed appeared to lead to nothing except wings with more cells. Judging by the oscillations of sound, these wings held far more captives than his.

If there had been the slightest hint of a way out, he'd have tried to break the guard's hold and make a break for it. The clammy touch of skin more amphibious than human made his skin crawl like nothing else. All three sentient species that coexisted on the planet were humanoid in shape and appearance, but the Hilruda were built to nightmare specifications.

Three fingers that ended in bulbous pads gave them an excellent grip. Their jaundiced skin was moist and clammy, like the rocks in which they preferred to make their home. Their eyes were small and beady, but their mouths were circular and fleshy, the only thing about the Hilruda that wasn't reminiscent of a long-dead cadaver. There was a reason people called them leeches, at least when no Hilruda was within earshot.

But the guards, for all that they were cadaverous, were taller and stronger than most humans, even Zerek, who was big for a human. Breaking away—even if he could—would gain him nothing.

Their journey ended at the edge of a circular open space, a thick layer of dirt covering the stone ground.

With a shove that seemed to be the guards' standard method, Zerek ended up on his hands and knees in the soil. A cheer rose up above, and Zerek pushed himself to his feet. Roughhewn stone walls surrounded most of the circle, with three other openings much like the one he'd arrived through.

The cheering came from a point well above his head, where several rows of seats ringed the stone circle. The seats were filled with more Hilruda than he'd ever seen in one place, each of them noxious in their fevered anticipation. A sneer curled his lip.

Ignore the crowd—they're a distraction.

After Zerek's cellmate had given him the obvious and extremely unhelpful advice of "don't lose," he'd gone on to provide more specific tips, in between bouts of wracking coughs that left him without breath to speak for several minutes. Zerek hadn't understood the crowd reference until now, as he hadn't wanted to push the man for explanations that would require more words. Distractions in a fight were bad news, but Zerek had trained a long time in preparation for this moment, even if he'd never quite expected it to come.

He shook out his arms, holding back a wince. That mold-sucking blight of a guard had likely left bruises from his grip.

"Greetings, my fellow Stony Gate patrons."

Trying to control his curiosity, Zerek shot his gaze around the stadium, searching for the speaker. The way the sound echoed and amplified around him, it wasn't easy to pinpoint, but the dramatic arm waving quickly drew his attention.

"We have a special treat for you today, fresh from his capture and sentencing yesterday. Zerek, the smuggling scourge of the human infestation, stands before you."

The cheering swelled, and the expression on the speaker's seamed face could only be interpreted as gleeful satisfaction. The speaker went on to announce the long list of Zerek's so-called crimes, but Zerek did his best to ignore it. He knew exactly what the fuck he'd done to foul up the Hilruda, and he needed to focus on surviving.

This time, the announcer addressed him directly. "Welcome to the pit, Zerek."

As much as he liked being a pain in the Hilruda's collective asses, he wasn't keen on his species being described as an infestation. If only his ancestors had known how much contempt the Hilruda held for them, they might have chosen a different planet to settle on.

Don't kill anyone. That'll just get you punished.

Zerek pulled his shoulders back and bounced on the balls of his feet, waiting. That was advice he'd actually been pleased about. Unless he ended up fighting one of the odious Hilruda. Nothing could hold him back in that case.

He'd heard rumors that some of the contests involved fighting beasts, and Zerek wouldn't sacrifice his life to save them, but he'd be happy if he could put them down without killing them. After all, they were here under duress just as much as he was. Still, he had to remember that even if he wasn't intending to kill anyone or anything, he had to assume that his opponents might have other ideas, and he needed to be prepared.

Asking for clarification of that tip, though, had been thwarted by a particularly vicious coughing fit that Zerek believed had ended in his cellmate spitting up blood. He'd merely waited, letting his cellmate regain his composure, and speak more only if he felt up to it.

Don't let them see your emotions.

That one didn't make sense at all, and he had wondered if his cellmate's illness had turned to delirium.

Where was his opponent? The announcer had finished his lengthy introduction, and the air in the area was thick with anticipation.

He'd figured out he wasn't going to be given a weapon, but he didn't know if weaponed fights were in the repertoire. He'd have to ask his cellmate when he returned.

A man appeared at one of the entrances, a guard pushing him with a lance. He shuffled into the light and the crowd roared, while Zerek did his best not to throw up. Not showing his emotions suddenly made sense. He didn't want the Hilruda to revel in his disgust and loathing, because there was no doubt they'd enjoy it. How was he supposed to fight a man who'd clearly been incarcerated for a long fucking time? Emaciated, pale, bruised, and obviously weak. This fight wasn't going to last long at all, and Zerek would have to be extremely careful to pull his blows, otherwise he might accidentally kill one of them. If he thought there was any way to avoid this travesty, he would do it in a heartbeat.

Then another five men in similar condition were prodded out into the arena. This time, Zerek couldn't hold in a glare, and he swept his angry gaze over the crowd before landing on the announcer.

The announcer met his gaze, eyes glittering with excitement. If the Hilruda were capable of grinning like mad men, the announcer undoubtedly would have done so. His next words were directed to Zerek as much as to the baying crowd.

"Six against one, a fitting challenge for the not so high and mighty Zerek. And all six have had two losses each. Losing to Zerek would make three, and we all know what that means."

The crowd fucking lost it.

Three losses gets you reassigned. Where to, no one knows, but it's a good bet it's worse than this shithole.

Zerek directed his focus to his opponents. Frail though they might be, all six of them had the look of desperation. Defeating them without killing would be no simple matter, even if he could live with condemning them to a third loss. He could afford a loss while he figured out a way to escape Stony Gate.

Plan firmly in mind, he strode to the middle of the arena. He would take immense pleasure in denying the crowd their tasteless spectacle.

"Do keep in mind, Zerek, that we expect a good show."

Shock made him look up. Clearly he had not done a good job of keeping his thoughts out of his expression, and the Hilruda had had generations to figure out how to read humans and manipulate them.

Glaring, he remained silent. He didn't give a fiery fuck what the Hilruda expected.

"If you lose, your companions in crime will be punished - severely. We've extended our hospitality so they can await their fate."

The cheering of the crowd was almost painful, and he closed his eyes at the threat against his crew. His cellmate had told the truth. Zerek hadn't been the only one captured.

Those men and women, handpicked by him over years, were the closest to family he had. Not that he expected the Hilruda to grant their freedom if Zerek won, but how could he condemn them to punishment which, based on the announcer's inflection, could well be fatal?

A gong resounded, almost ear-shattering in its intensity, and Zerek's eyes flew open just in time to see six determined, but sickly, men rush him.

Bracing himself, he was able to avoid the first few blows, but with six men to deal with, he couldn't track all of them, nor could he face all of them. A kick to the back of his leg sent him off balance, but he seized the moment to take out one of his opponents. Grabbing the man closest to him, he tucked the man to his chest and they both fell to the ground. Since Zerek did his best to control the fall, he landed on top of the man with a sickening snap. A fraction of a second was enough to tell Zerek that it wasn't his bone that broke, although he'd taken a few blows to his chest as they went down. Rolling to the side, he dislodged a man who had pounced onto his back, and sprang up again. The man he'd fallen on drew in a deep breath, clutched his leg, and howled.

Zerek danced around, the five men in his sightline again, however briefly. Swarming him in a melee appeared to be their strategy, and there was a good chance they'd win simply by overwhelming him. But attacking them, despite the stakes, felt so wrong. The man he'd shaken off his back got back to his feet, but appeared slow and unfocused.

They converged again, fists at the ready, and this time, Zerek lunged at the dazed one and slammed a fist into his jaw. Zerek's longer reach gave him the advantage and the malnourished man dropped to the sand, hopefully only unconscious and not dead. The Hilruda were going to pay for this, if he had anything to say about it.

Four of them were still enough to get him on the ground, one of them getting in a lucky hit on the raised knot on his skull where his captors had hit him. Vision blurring, he curled up, trying to protect his pounding skull, while he concentrated on stopping the world from spinning. He grunted under the blows that fell on him, strong enough to hurt and bruise, but somehow not powerful enough to do any real damage. Lack of experience caused them to get in each other's way. It had been clear from the first second that none of them were trained fighters, whatever experience they'd gained in the pit.

As soon as his equilibrium settled, he struggled to a position with more leverage. An opening appeared between two attackers and he lunged through it, shaking off men who weren't physically well enough to react as quickly as Zerek could.

Whirling, he slammed one of them in the ribs. His blow opened a series of half-healed parallel scabs that looked like claw marks, lending credence to the rumor that the pit fighting included battles against animals.

The third man dropped to the ground, arms wrapped around himself as he struggled to breathe. If Zerek hadn't snapped ribs with that punch, the guy might still be in the fight, if he couldn't get the other three down.

Fortunately, although Zerek hated the thought, two of the three had already expended the last of their energy. Zerek tried to pull his blows, aiming to incapacitate rather than truly injure, but a couple more broken bones put those two out of the fight, leaving him one last opponent.

This man's expression was almost feral as he bared his teeth and circled Zerek. This man had likely won several bouts along with his two losses. If starvation and poor conditions hadn't made him thin and stringy, he'd have been almost Zerek's size and likely bulk.

If this man had gotten close enough to him in the early stages of the fight, Zerek would likely be more damaged than he was right now. Both of them were tired, though. Tired enough that Zerek might lose, if he made a mistake.

Only one solution came to mind. He had to go on the offensive, take advantage of his healthy status, and take this guy down as quick as possible.

Zerek charged, sweeping the man off his feet with his heavier bulk. They slammed to the ground and grappled with each other. For a few alarming moments, Zerek ended up on his back, wrestling against two hands gripped firmly around his throat. Just as his vision started to go black, Zerek broke the guy's hold and flipped them. Finesse lost, he punched and punched, the man's lips splitting under his fists, teeth opening cuts on Zerek's knuckles, until finally the man went limp beneath him.

Horrified, Zerek slumped to the side, and waited endless moments before his final opponent dragged in a breath.

He stumbled to his feet, the announcer's words and the cheers of the crowd merely noise in the background. Surveying the damage he'd done to his fellow humans, there was no sense of victory. He'd been an animal, and the Hilruda had done that to him. Disgust and a renewed determination to make the Hilruda pay filled him. He fought desperately to keep his horror off his face, because he now understood why he'd been told to keep his emotions under wraps. Knowing how much he hated himself for what he'd done would be like a sweet, gooey dessert after the hearty meal of his battle to the Hilruda spectators.

The guards half-led, half-dragged him back to his cell. The fight, or perhaps fighting, with a concussion, had taken a lot out of him, because he'd never felt so drained.

He sank dizzily onto the uncomfortable cot as the guards locked the door behind him.

"Hey, fellow cellmate, are you there? I won." At what cost, he wasn't sure, but at least he'd saved his crew. "Thanks for your help."

There was no reply. If the guy was as sick as he'd sounded earlier, he probably slept more than he was awake. Zerek didn't try to speak again, because they both needed to rest.

CHAPTER TWO

The ache from a series of bruises on his ribs made sleep on the thin mattress impossible, but exhaustion warred with discomfort and he dozed fitfully. Zerek was sore, starving, chilled to his bones, and he'd only endured one day of Stony Gate's hospitality. One fight. Which he'd won, thanks to a few additional tips from his cell mate, but he hadn't expected his opponents to be six half-starved prisoners who attempted to swarm him to take him down. The victory had cost him something inside, and the only respite from the guilt was that the pit fights weren't to the death. He'd not had to kill those poor, desperate souls.

Even during the few snatches of sleep, despair tried to clutch at him. The guards had paraded him in front of the crowd, the prison administrator crowing his name and applauding his capture. The cheers that rose from the Hilruda spectators held a vicious joy.

Aside from a better idea of how the pit fights were organized, the only other information he'd gleaned was the path from his cell to the pit. If his crew had been captured, they weren't housed in the same wing as him, nor had they been present at his fight. Most of the cells in his section were empty, aside from his one companion, and the sudden light from the guards meant he'd been temporarily blinded. Escape wasn't going to be as easy as he'd thought.

He shifted again and sat up, the motion making his head spin again, but he tried to ignore it. Without the ability to sleep properly, this might be his best night... day... he didn't even know what time it was. After the fight, his clothes were more ragged and stiff with dried blood, most of it from his opponents. Each day he stayed, each day he fought, he ran the risk of losing the clothes he came in with or being injured. Injured worse.

As much as he hated the thought, he needed to get out of here, however blind he'd be. He ran his fingers over the loose stitching at the hem of his

9

shirt and started picking.

Every bit of metal had been stripped from him before his incarceration, but Zerek believed in being prepared. One of his most prized and expensive purchases, one of the few exchanges he'd made strictly for himself, was a set of thieves tools made out of hardened quelar bones. The large horned reptiles were notoriously difficult to catch, but their bones were sturdier than most metal and, true to claims, missed the prison scans for metal objects.

Once the seam on his shirt had opened enough, he pulled out a pouch, tiny enough to miss the invasive and rude physical searches for weapons. This was his way out.

An explosion of motion, rather than sound, had him looking up just as the door to his cell burst open. With a reflex borne of years of hiding in the shadows, Zerek unobtrusively tucked the pouch in his waistband as he pretended to cower back against the wall.

Three hooded figures approached, and two of them grabbed his arms. They were about the same size as Zerek, which wasn't common. He was big for a human.

"What are you doing?" What vital information was he missing? Had the Hilruda somehow found out about his contraband? Or was there something besides the fights that prisoners were required to participate in, something he wasn't aware of?

"Shut up if you want to leave here alive."

Prudence made Zerek comply, but the unusual musky scent and strange sibilance on the figure's pronunciation of "shut" told Zerek that this wasn't a rescue from his crew.

They hustled him out of the cell and steered him in a direction away from the pits.

"Wait." Zerek kept his voice low, but dug his heels in as best he could, since his sudden movements had made him dizzy and he didn't want these newcomers to realize how rotten he felt.

"What?" The same figure, who was possibly the leader, answered with clear annoyance.

"If you're getting me out of here, we need to take my friend." Assuming this was a rescue attempt was a bit of a gamble, but his entire life had been a calculated risk, and the sick man in the next cell had been more helpful than he'd needed to be for a stranger.

There was an extended pause. "Stay quiet."

One of the figures backtracked and did something with the lock, faster than Zerek would have been with his bone tools.

Far too soon, the hooded figure emerged empty handed and shaking his head. Zerek broke free of his captors... rescuers... whoever... and dashed into the cell.

An emaciated dirty man lay on the pallet, eyes open and staring. A quick touch of his wrist told Zerek that he'd been dead for hours, probably had been dead when Zerek had returned from the fight, explaining why he hadn't answered Zerek when he'd thanked him for his helpful insights.

Bilge-bathing swamp rats.

Zerek didn't fight when his new companions grabbed his arms again. So soon after the pit, he didn't have the energy to break free unless his life depended on it.

"Follow quietly or we'll bind and gag you." Zerek was familiar with the tone the leader used, he used it himself when he was tired of dealing with nonsense.

For the time being, he'd accompany this merry little band, play the good little rescued captive. Until he figured out what was going on. Then he'd escape. He was good at escape, and he had a little revenge to perpetrate. At least the four of them had a better chance if they needed to fight their way out of Stony Gate, and when Zerek finally took his leave, he might have a better chance at swiping some of their supplies.

The coffin-like wooden box Zerek had lain in for three days now jolted along some seriously rough terrain. He'd been given regular breaks for food, water, and to take care of business, but this last stretch had been longer than the rest, and rattling around in the box wasn't doing his bladder any favors.

Some fucking "rescue." During the previous day, he'd begun to believe this was a form of torture cooked up by the Hilruda. He'd heard they got off in a serious way on people's pain, and if this was an example, he could well believe it. Each time he'd been released from his temporary prison—as a cell it was worse than the one he'd left behind in Stony Gate—his muscles protested more, his eyes had more difficulty adjusting, and the stiffness in his joints left him hobbled and wincing, dreading yet another stint in the box. The three people remained hooded, preventing any chance at identification.

The first day, he'd pounded weakly on the lid, screaming questions as loud as he could. That hadn't lasted long, because he irritated the leader good, judging by the way the box had been flung on the ground with little concern for his injuries.

The lid flipped up, a torch in his eyes keeping the leader's face in shadow. "You'll draw unwanted attention."

Zerek assumed the mutinous expression on his face hadn't gone over well, because he'd been forcibly sedated. Once he'd awoken, several hours had passed and he'd learned his lesson. If he had to escape from these fuckers, he'd miss his chance if he was drugged into unconsciousness. Whatever drug they'd given him had been the worst sedative ever—he didn't feel one bit rested after he'd awoken.

Instead of concentrating on how much he had to piss, he checked—for the thousandth time—that his lock pick set was still tucked in his waistband. Then, starting at his feet and working upward, he flexed and released his muscles. It wasn't much, but it was all that kept him from being crippled each time they let him out of the box.

He resolutely didn't think about his crew, and how each hour on their journey, they might be captive at Stony Gate, fighting in the pit and losing hope, drop by drop.

Just when the fullness of his bladder became painful, they came to a stop. Unceremoniously, the lid was lifted and they tipped him out. He rolled to a stop on the floor and concentrated on not embarrassing himself. Groaning, he pushed himself to his feet and blinked, nearly blinded by the daylight. Figures surrounded him, nothing more than dark shapes. Moisture gathered in his eyes, and he wiped at them furiously, to clear his vision.

Finally, his eyes adjusted. This time, no one was hooded. Distinctive, yet attractive, mottled skin, mouths that looked like they had too many teeth, and tiny noses told him exactly who'd rescued him.

Kadrussians. It figured.

"I want to know what is going on." A cramp hit his midsection, and heat swept across his cheeks. "But first, where the fuck are your facilities?"

The biggest Kadrussian waved a hand and nodded, which was enough for one of his "rescuers" to lead him none too gently out of the room. He'd at least been able to pick those three out of the group, because they still wore the unobtrusive, sack-like robes they wore when they'd pulled him out of his cell. The leader of that little threesome definitely ranked lower than the big Kadrussian who'd given orders with nothing more than a gesture.

With a tiny bit of privacy in the facility, Zerek leaned against the wall, shivering from intense relief bordering on orgasmic. Being on his feet again was a small joy as well. Given the length of their trip, he had to be deep in Kadrussian territory. Although he had dealings with several Kadrussians, including that triple-cursed Gress, he didn't recognize any of the men. He did have enough sense to know the big guy, the one that had at least fifty pounds and a few inches on him, had to be a clan leader. Which clan, he wasn't sure. The Kadrussians had a way to tell clan members apart, but unless Zerek was told or knew where he was geographically, he couldn't guess which clan's hospitality he was...enduring.

Like any other human on the planet, Zerek had grown up hearing stories about the Great Journey and the Bitter Silence. The Great Journey spoke of the human migration to this planet on huge spaceships that supposedly orbited to this day. The Great Journey stories spoke of hope, of sharing a planet in harmony alongside two alien species, living a more pure, lower-tech life. Aside from some unflattering comparisons to animal species for both the Hilruda and Kadrussians, those stories were good. Lower-tech wasn't no-tech, though, and the human immigrants continued to receive regular supplies and support from the empire.

Then, about three generations ago, the empire was torn apart by a vicious civil war. Humans lost all communication with the rest of their species, and remained at the mercy of the aliens occupying the same planet. The Kadrussians, ever reclusive and territorial, simply withdrew deeper into their clan lands. The Hilruda, though, had no mercy, and took advantage of the situation in a way no one predicted.

Zerek liked to think if he'd been alive before the Bitter Silence, he'd have intuited the Hilruda danger, but maybe the threat of technology, weapons, and troops from the human empire had enabled them to better hide their true nature.

"Are you done yet? You can play with yourself later." Impatient banging accompanied the words.

Zerek rolled his eyes. What was the world coming to, that a man couldn't take a piss in peace? True, he'd zoned out a bit, but sure as shit wasn't rubbing one out after being kidnapped and locked in a box for the better part of three days. So, he finished up and exited the facilities.

His escort was no more gentle on the return to the group who waited for him.

They stood in silence for several long moments, long enough for Zerek to become aware of just how rank his clothes were. He needed to get this meeting moving along, because if he'd truly been rescued, they'd better be providing some fresh clothes and a bath.

He zeroed in on the big guy; no point in talking to underlings, after all. "Good job, sneaking into Stony Gate like that. Quite the feat. I applaud your men and your plan, but if your men had bothered listening to anything I said, they made a mistake."

"And what mistake would that be?" A flash of fang in the clan leader's mouth explained the heavier sibilance on the s. He'd heard stories about Kadrussians who were permanently fanged, but time would tell if they held any truth.

In any case, paying attention to the clan leader was no hardship. Big, sexy, and alluring in a way few men were, in Zerek's opinion.

"I'm assuming this uncomfortable jaunt was meant to be a rescue attempt. I'm not Kadrussian." He paused for a moment to let them snort at his obvious joke. "I'm just a humble smuggler. Your men must have been after someone much more important."

Humble was a lie. He was a fucking awesome smuggler, recent incarceration notwithstanding, but he was still a nobody. Like most of the humans left to lick the boots of those mud licking Hilruda.

Another negligent wave of the Kadrussian's hand sent his three rescuers/captors out of the room. Zerek couldn't tell if the remaining four bystanders were bodyguards, advisors, or merely disinterested observers.

"Have a seat. Would you like something to eat or drink?"

"Really? A greeting ritual?" Zerek huffed in exasperation, but his stomach snarled in protest. "Fine. Yes, thank you."

Good thing the big guy was hot, or Zerek would be even more pissed at this delay. He scratched at his chest, the itch something he could no longer ignore and grimaced. Any minute now he'd drop to his knees and beg for a bath. He was amazed any of them could stand to be in the same room as him. Zerek could hardly stand himself and he was stuck in his own skin.

Zerek followed the leader to a table in the corner by a window. A quick glance outside only confirmed they were fucking far from Stony Gate, three days' journey to be precise. They were high up, but there was only greenery and mountains as far as the eye could see. Any landmarks he'd use to determine location would be at ground level, under the canopy of trees. It ruled out the territory of at least three Kadrussian clans, who lived underground, but there were seven or eight others that held territory like this.

The leader took the chair in the corner, giving him sight lines for the entire room. With a curl of his lip, Zerek took the other chair. He did not enjoy exposing his back, but he wasn't the one making the rules here. Concessions needed to be made, and unfortunately, he'd be the one making them. Zerek sat and waited without saying a word.

Refreshments arrived with surprising swiftness, and the other clan members melted away. They were still in the room, giving credence to the bodyguard theory, but far enough away that they couldn't hear conversation at the table. Not unless he or the clan leader chose to shout.

His last shred of politeness dissolved in the face of refreshments that weren't trail rations or moldy prison food. He fell on the beautifully displayed finger foods like a ravening beast.

The clan leader allowed him to stuff his face until he finally took a breath to swallow and savor.

"My name is Essian."

Zerek choked and coughed, crumbs flying. He knew who Essian was. Leader of the only clan whose name literally translated to "snake", and often he was referred to as The Snake in a fearful manner. The clans generally kept to themselves, and ruled as autonomous states, but if the Kadrussians had a royal line, the crown prince sat before him. But to genuflect or anything else was out of the question. He'd done enough of that under Hilruda control; he'd become a smuggler to avoid that shit. He'd faced the pit despite his fears; no way was he letting The Snake see any fear.

"Pleased to meet you, I'm Brandos." Zerek hoped his exaggerated air of boredom and fake name fooled Essian.

Essian let out a lilting hiss, a Kadrussian's version of laughing. Nope. The Snake saw through him. Which Zerek found enticing when he should have been apprehensive.

"Do not lie to me, Zerek. It does not become you."

Zerek raised an eyebrow. "I'm a smuggler. I lie for a living. And what makes you think I'm this Zerek fellow?"

An intent stare from golden eyes was Essian's only response. Zerek shrugged. It was worth a try, but his curiosity nagged. If Essian knew who he was, he'd had his men break into Stony Gate for the express purpose of extracting him. Perhaps one day, Zerek would appreciate that, but that would depend on why.

"What am I doing here?" The view out the window made more sense, now that he knew he was in Serpentes territory. Those three minions had made good time, especially with him as a burden.

Essian waited, and Zerek stared. Essian had gorgeous coloring, some of the most attractive he'd seen on a Kadrussian. Various shades of bronze and copper, threaded with gold, formed patterns that blended and wove over his skin. In the sunlight, all of his exposed skin had a faint metallic gloss, and if he'd come across Essian under any other circumstances, he'd have reached out and touched.

The man was broad, muscular, and had an air about him that made Zerek want to puff up his chest. Sometimes, Zerek wondered if there was an explanation for the fact that three vastly different species evolved similar builds and forms, but if that information ever existed, it was probably long gone after the Bitter Silence. His grandfather, who'd been a biologist before the Bitter Silence, had tried to share his knowledge with Zerek, but he'd been too young to understand. After his grandfather's death, there was no more time for stories and abstract concepts. Survival had ruled, now Zerek was a simple smuggler with no theories of his own.

Nevertheless, he found the Kadrussians, this one more so than any other, far more attractive than the cadaverous Hilruda. Information he intended to keep to himself, as was only prudent. Whatever Essian wanted, Zerek didn't want to undermine his position.

Essian flicked out a bifurcated tongue, scenting the air briefly before tucking it back into his mouth. Again, Zerek caught another flash of fang, supposedly a physical manifestation of virility and power. He could well believe it. According to his sources, the fangs only dropped during battle or mating. Given Essian's relaxed appearance, Zerek could only assume the fangs were permanent, as he didn't seem poised to kill or fuck anyone just now.

And if the thought of Essian demonstrating some of that virility right now, well...Zerek shifted and got another whiff of his noxious scent. Maybe no virility demonstrations until he'd scrubbed a layer or twelve off his skin and wouldn't be too humiliated to participate. Or, until he'd rested enough to get an erection. If he wasn't so exhausted, he'd already be chubbing up, given how much he wanted to lick Essian's bronzed skin.

It didn't escape his attention that Essian hadn't made any effort to answer his question, but volunteering information wasn't in his temperament or job description, so Zerek was content to eat and stare at his incredibly attractive host.

Finally, the food was gone and Zerek wanted a bath and a change of clothes far more than he wanted to play this game with Essian.

"Even if I was Zerek, I'm still a smuggler. I'm nothing. I never deal directly with clan leaders. Why did you bring me here?"

Kadrussians didn't have any body hair—another trait they shared with the reptiles people so often compared them to, so Essian couldn't raise an eyebrow, but there was no mistaking his smug expression. Zerek replayed his words and scowled. He must be in worse shape than he'd realized, because he'd as good as admitted he was indeed Zerek, as well as knowing Essian was a clan leader.

"As it happens, I'm in need of a smuggler."

"What? Why?" Zerek had deals and relationships with a number of Kadrussians, they were part of his vast network, but this didn't make any sense.

"The Hilruda have become a menace that needs to be dealt with."

Zerek touched his head where a small knot still lay under the skin from his concussion a few days earlier. It had scrambled his brains good, and was improving with a distressing lack of speed.

"Need to be dealt with?" Anger chased away his confusion. "They've effectively turned my people into fucking slaves in less than a hundred years. And my people were space travelers. Why are you just figuring this out now? Why didn't you help us?"

Essian shrugged. "Many reasons. Our clans are... insular, isolated even from each other. The leaders often rely on tradition to govern, but our traditions didn't change with the appearance of your people on this planet, and likewise didn't change when your people were left without support from your empire, vulnerable to the Hilruda."

Zerek thumped a fist on the table.

"Why the fuck do you think I smuggle in the first place? I don't just smuggle goods, you know. I try to get as many people out of Hilruda hands as I can. I know what the stakes are, but I'm one man. I'm a fucking criminal, a fucking good one." He also had more pride than was good for him. "But I'm one man trying to stop the planet from turning."

Movement from the corner of his eye showed the bodyguards—which he'd foolishly forgotten about—take a few steps toward the table. With some effort, Zerek projected calm, even if fury still seethed in his heart.

"Our clan leaders thought the Hilruda would be content with dominion over humankind, but they grow greedy and encroach on our territory more each year. They ignore treaties where they can, and they flout our laws and customs just shy of the point of a declaration of war. Probably because they don't know our numbers, but I do."

Zerek wondered at the inflection Essian put on "clan leaders". He recalled Essian had only been clan leader a few months, since the recent death of his father, and he wondered if the odd emphasis meant Essian didn't yet feel like a clan leader, or if he'd disagreed with their stance on the Hilruda matter.

"And? Do you outnumber them?"

Silence reigned for several moments, and Zerek had his answer. Essian was in an unenviable position. The Kadrussians had watched in silence while a once proud and accomplished people had been ground into paste under the withered foot of the Hilruda, and Essian knew the Kadrussians were next.

"Anyway, that doesn't explain why you went to such lengths to break me out of Stony Gate. I was planning to escape." Eventually. "Can't run a smuggling ring from inside that place."

This time, Essian's expression reminded him of an old wise man, exasperated by a youngster's naivety—despite the fact that Zerek was probably only a year or two younger than Essian.

"You don't understand," Essian continued. "Your people call the Hilruda leeches and vampires, but those epithets have more truth than you realize. They feed on the energy of living things. In the pit, the fighters generate huge amounts of energy."

Zerek's eyes widened as the reason for the pit fights, and even the way the prisoners were treated, became clear.

The clan leader wasn't finished, though. "Yes, the Hilruda feed on the emotion you expend in the ring. Feed on the high of the spectators too, but for non-Hilruda, they take something from you each time. It weakens you, diminishes you. Takes a long time to recover, but if you lose too much energy or too often, there is no recovery. It's the reason no one lasts long in Stony Gate. You lose too many times, and you'll end up a dead husk. But it's inevitable that you'll lose, because each time you fight, win or lose, they take a little more of your life force."

Nausea boiled in his gut, making him regret how much he'd eaten. No wonder he was in such rough shape. He'd assumed it had been an unfortunate reaction to the sedative, but it was a reaction to—he gagged slightly—feeding the Hilruda.

Gulping at the fruit juice remaining in his cup, he tried to calm his roiling stomach. That information put a new spin on the pit fighting prohibition against killing one's opponent. Zerek had been so relieved. Taking someone's life wasn't easy, and he'd been worried he'd have to kill to survive. A tiny sliver of him had applauded their fucking mercy. It wasn't mercy at all—it was food rationing. Those putrid turd swallowers.

"So, what's your plan?" Essian had to have one. It was the only explanation for Zerek's presence.

"As I said, I need a smuggler."

"What are we smuggling?"

"Me."

Cryptic. And somehow the sexy bastard knew that his answer would tweak Zerek's curiosity. Too bad he was fading fast. Exhaustion rarely won out over his willpower—yet another indignity he could lay at the Hilruda's door.

"I don't see any bags. Do these plans involve leaving in the next twelve hours?"

"Supplies are prepared, but tomorrow or the next day will be soon enough."

Good. If he was smuggling Essian anywhere, he'd have plenty of time to ferret out the whys and wherefores.

"Not sure how we'll figure out a percentage of you." Zerek had a couple of ideas he wouldn't mind testing out, though. "But I'm sure we can come to an agreement about a fair and reasonable fee."

"Gratitude for the rescue isn't enough?" Essian flashed his fang again, but it didn't faze Zerek. Biting Zerek wouldn't get Essian any closer to his goal, since Kadrussian venom would either kill Zerek or put him out of commission for a very long time.

"Gratitude doesn't buy food or shelter." Zerek wasn't going to push the issue. Gratitude for his rescue wasn't reason enough, but having an important clan leader in his debt might be worth more than gems. "I'm in. On one condition. You send your men back to Stony Gate and get my crew out of there." He wasn't going to let them rot in there any longer than he had to, especially now that he knew what they'd have to endure. And for each fight they were in, Zerek was going to break one of Gress's bones as payback for his betrayal. Once this job for Essian was complete, Zerek wasn't going to rest until he tracked down Gress.

"Your crew wasn't captured. Only you were."

"Are you sure? One of the other prisoners said he'd heard some of the guards talking about it." And that pit whore of an announcer had used his crew as leverage, but telling Essian that would be like exposing his vulnerable belly to a predator.

Essian shook his head. "Lies. Or misinformation."

"How would you know?"

"We rescued you from the heart of Hilruda territory, in one of their most heavily guarded buildings less than two days after your sentencing. I think you can trust my sources."

Cracking his knuckles, Zerek considered that. Leaving his crew hung out to dry was unacceptable, but there was a certain logic to Essian's statement. And he was a three days' journey from Stony Gate as it was. Trust he would, for now.

"Then have your men deliver a message." If they truly hadn't been captured, he had to warn them about Gress.

"That I can do. Shall we make plans?"

Plans would be smart, and under normal circumstances, Zerek would never have agreed to do a job like this before knowing the full details of what was expected. But the very real possibility he was about to collapse in front of this powerful, and unfortunately attractive, clan leader superseded his normal caution. If it turned out later that Essian wasn't bargaining in good faith, well, he'd worry about that later. Zerek stood on legs that wobbled slightly.

"Nope. Have someone show me to a bedchamber. I need a bath, fresh clothes, and sleep before we start making plans."

The next morning, Zerek emerged from a bed chamber that had been surprisingly well-appointed, considering his complete lack of clan status.

But he was washed and wearing comfortable clothes that weren't soaked in blood. As for being well-rested, he was close. Essian must have been telling the truth about the Hilruda draining him, because weakness and fatigue lingered like an unwelcome house guest.

A few steps down the hall stood another guard, a reminder that Zerek wasn't a trusted member of the household. Zerek didn't blame them a bit; he wouldn't trust him either.

"You. Where's Essian?"

The guard snarled at Zerek's imperious tone, but beckoned for him to follow. Zerek didn't care—at all—what anyone thought of his attitude. He'd made a career of giving the finger to the Hilruda. A clan leader like Essian might be impressive, but Zerek wasn't bowing to anyone. Humans had done more than their fair share of that since the Bitter Silence.

When they stopped, it was outside a different chamber than the cavernous reception room from the previous day. He was forced to wait several minutes while a few guards conversed in hissing, spitting undertones.

Stifling the temptation to just barrel through the door, since he wasn't a threat to Essian, he tapped his foot as he waited. Avoiding the authorities required infinite patience, but Zerek wasn't in the middle of a job yet, and his patience was entirely reserved for work.

"Can we get this done already? We're wasting hours here." Depending on the scope of the job and what Essian deemed appropriate as supplies, they'd likely be able to get going today.

None of Essian's clan people were thrilled with him, but a tall, imperious woman, whose skin was covered in beautiful patterns of green and blue, opened the door. Zerek strode inside. The first thing he saw was Essian seated at a table covered in semi-opaque sheet maps. Zerek smiled until he noticed the bed.

Essian's bedchamber. The intimacy of that, even if there was no chance of anything sexual occurring, unsettled and aroused him. The skin on his nape crawled. He and Essian appeared to be the only occupants of the room. Unless Essian intended to seduce him—unlikely—the clans' people wouldn't leave them unattended.

As much as he hated the thought of surveillance he couldn't spot, a tiny, wicked part of him gloried in the idea of Essian taking him in that sumptuous bed, in front of those unseen observers.

When his cock started to respond, he grimaced. Contrary, troublesome, brainless piece of flesh. Not that he wasn't pleased he'd rested well enough for his cock to start working again as expected, but he ruthlessly tamped down his desire. He'd be able to fly before he'd be able to fulfill his sexual fantasies.

Zerek cleared his throat, and although Essian's attention appeared to be firmly on the map in front of him, a flicker of tongue and a gesture to a chair said otherwise. He slid into the chair and Essian slid the map around so they could both see it.

"I need to travel to five clan strongholds."

"And what do you need me for? Why not take some of your bodyguards or a small armed force or whatever you've got?"

Essian pointed at five clan lands, all of which bordered Hilruda territory, and suddenly part of this ridiculous scheme made sense. All five lands had regular intrusions from the Hilruda, and Essian needed a way to get there without the Hilruda finding out. They were also the primary clans that Zerek had dealings with, and he didn't think that was coincidental.

"You're very well informed." Which didn't ease his nerves, although he admired Essian's resources and thoroughness.

"I try." If anyone else had said that, they'd have been unbearably smug to the point Zerek would be tempted to punch them, but Essian had already proved he had good reason for his arrogance.

"How come you were able to get into Stony Gate, but not stealth your way into the other clans?" Zerek rubbed the back of his neck, still stiff after a full night's sleep on a proper bed.

"It took months to get the right information for Stony Gate, and the Hilruda have no reason to suspect that I was the one behind your escape. That means whatever conclusion they draw from your absence will not be the correct one."

"And exactly what conclusion..." Nope. He was done with this idiocy. "Essian, if you want my fucking help, just tell me what you need. If we keep dancing around the issue, we're going to be here until we die of old age."

Essian looked up, tongue flickering out again. At least Zerek had managed to say his piece without sounding too antagonistic. No one was springing from secret doorways to arrest him, nor was Essian calling for his guards.

"Are you always this impatient?"

He was going to get a cramp in his face from suppressing the eye rolling. "Are you always this evasive? Because here's the thing. I risk my neck every time I take a job. And now that I'm a fugitive, it's going to be even worse. I need every relevant scrap of information to keep us both out of trouble, and you're not being forthcoming. At all."

There was no reason to tell Essian that he enjoyed the danger almost as much as he enjoyed the sense of rightness about what he did. When he'd awoken with a familiar tingle of excitement in his belly, he knew he'd be pushing to leave as soon as was reasonable.

Silence hung between them, and Zerek took the time to study Essian's features. He'd had more exposure to Kadrussians than most humans, but he still wasn't always able to read their facial expressions. Similar physiology didn't equate to similar mentality, a theory proved out a hundred times over by the Hilruda, but his limited knowledge of the Kadrussians led him to believe that at least some of their goals, morals, and emotions ran in close parallel.

Something about the clan leader made him seem trustworthy. Zerek had made more than his fair share of judgements based on gut feelings, but he never liked to rely on them. In this case, he might not have any choice. If he was smart, he'd find a way out of this, but the adrenaline high of something new, and the odd, compelling pull of Essian's confident aura weighed more heavily in favor of going along with this plan, whatever it was.

"No armed guards. Just you and me. We can't appear to be an invading force. The Hilruda can't know what I'm doing. And if possible, I'd like to avoid the other clanspeople until I've had a chance to meet with the leaders." Essian's golden-eyed gaze flickered over the room, and Zerek knew the glance was not random. Although he didn't know why Essian would hint there were listeners, or rather, confirm the presence Zerek had already intuited, he understood instinctively that getting the whole story would have to wait.

"Tricky. Are you sure you don't want a burglar for this?"

This time, there was no mistaking Essian's expression—mocking disbelief.

Zerek snorted. "Fine, fine. I've done my share of stealing. But sneaking you into a clan leader's bedroom when I've never even scoped out the place? As a human, I'd stand out too much."

Not as much as he would have ten years ago, when he'd started smuggling especially mistreated humans out of Hilruda territory. Most of them lived in Kadrussian territories, but that didn't translate to unlimited human access to all clan properties.

"No, no. That level is not required. We just need to make it to the stronghold of each clan leader unhindered and unknown."

"And, what, you're just going to walk up to the door and ask for entrance?"

"Is that enough detail?" Essian didn't bother answering his question. Guess that was another detail that he'd find out later... if he needed to know.

As long as Essian didn't expect to get skewered by a rival clan leader, then yeah, Zerek probably had enough to go on. For now. He tilted a head toward the large packs sitting on the other side of the bed.

"Those our supplies?"

"Indeed. I took the liberty of having them prepared."

Uh-huh. "I need a complete inventory of what's in them. And I need some time with these maps."

Essian pushed the maps toward him. "I'll get you a list. I have a few things that I need to take care of before we leave. Tell the guard outside when you've decided on a departure time. There are facilities through the second door."

Zerek couldn't help himself. He stared at Essian's strong backside as he strode regally out of his bedroom. Once he'd shut the door behind him, Zerek slumped slightly, the encounter more stressful than he'd realized, primarily because he'd been desperate to control his unruly cock. Essian looked good and smelled even better.

Idly stroking the map, he let his gaze drift around the room, trying to get a sense of who Essian was. How much action the bed got. There wasn't any evidence of a second person occupying the room, but then, the Kadrussians were quite closemouthed about their sexual and mating practices. He'd seen a number of them naked, and was as sure as he could be without intimate inspection that Kadrussian and human parts would fit together just fine.

As a smuggler, there'd never been a good reason to ask for those kinds of details. As a man, he'd wanted to pry, and never so much as since he'd laid eyes on Essian, but he never got any sense the men he came in contact with were interested in him sexually. Not even Essian, much to his dismay.

Being left alone in Essian's bedroom removed any doubt that the room was under surveillance, and discouraged him from getting up to poke around in Essian's things. Test out his bed. Check for evidence of sexual activity.

He shook himself. Finish the job. Then worry about fucking. Mixing the two only led to trouble.

Ignoring a cock that had been semi-aroused the whole morning wasn't easy, but he had a job to plan, one that might be more dangerous than anything he'd done before. He needed all available blood in his brain. After a few minutes of concentrating on the maps, the lust cleared from his mind and let him do what he did best.

CHAPTER THREE

Sweat trickled down Zerek's back. The day was unexpectedly hot after spending two days in an underground tunnel leading away from the center of Serpentes territory.

That tunnel had been a real kick in the balls. "If you knew about all these secret tunnels, why am I here again?"

It was the first time since they'd started their journey that either one of them had touched on any of the super-secret things Essian was hiding from him. Under the confines of the tunnel, he'd felt eyes on them, same as those unseen watchers in Essian's bedroom. Presumably Essian would be just as happy to keep those secrets as long as Zerek would let him.

"I only know the tunnels in my territory. If there are secret ways into other clan lands, you would know more than I would."

Mollified, Zerek let them cover a little more ground, the silence broken only by their footfalls, softened by years of vegetation turned to mulch under the canopy of the trees above.

He shifted the bulky pack, wishing for about the millionth time that he'd been given a chance to pick up some of his own equipment. Stories of the Great Journey told how humans desired a world with less technology in it. Closer to nature. A purer existence. Until the Bitter Silence, when the Hilruda outlawed it, most humans retained some technology. Zerek had inherited some of it, hoarded and hidden, and one piece in particular made lengthy journeys such as this quicker and easier than acting as a beast of burden.

There were days of travel ahead of him, and he was just going to have to tough it out. Wouldn't be the first time, but that didn't mean he liked the idea.

The worst part would be finding a way to take care of certain needs without Essian knowing. Watching Essian's muscular ass flex as he walked in front wasn't doing him any favors. At least in the tunnels, the light had been too dim for Zerek to become distracted.

He quickened his pace to draw alongside his companion. As much as he wanted to interrogate Essian, they had another day's travel before they reached the next clan's territory. Half a day from there to the stronghold. Pressuring Essian to talk might only make for an awkward, uncomfortable trip.

Several minutes later, Essian cleared his throat. "Shortly before your people were cut off from the empire, our historians discovered a previously unknown prophecy in documents almost completely deteriorated."

"Prophecy?" Zerek couldn't keep the incredulity from his tone.

"Once, long before humans arrived, clan leaders relied on seers for advice. The seers dreamed of futures, both immutable and mutable. Much to the dishonor of my people, the seers were savagely murdered in an attempt to unite the clans by force. The attempt failed, but it's the reason the clans generally keep to themselves."

Zerek wasn't sure what to make of the whole seer business. Wasn't something he believed in, but Essian's conviction was unmistakable. Instead, he made a murmur of assent. Whether or not this story had any relevance to their journey, Zerek didn't mind. He enjoyed the lyrical way Essian spoke, and there was still plenty of time for information sharing.

"Historians did their best to preserve the documents, but so many of them were dismissed as nonsense. Except, once the humans showed up many of the more unbelievable prophesies made more sense."

An unexpected laugh bubbled up in Zerek's throat. Essian shot him a curious glance.

"Sorry. Just imagining the day we landed and a bunch of your historians collectively saying so that's what *falling from the sky meant.*" After all, humans had now spent more time under Hilruda rule than they had spent on the planet before the Bitter Silence. They were a fairly new addition to the planet.

Much to Zerek's pleasure, Essian gave his hissing version of a laugh. "I assure you, the prophecies aren't usually that straightforward."

Whether he believed or not, Zerek wanted to hear more. "What happened?"

"There was a revised interest in trying to decode the prophesies, another flurry of interest after the Bitter Silence. One of them speaks of—we think—the necessity of joining the clans. Otherwise, we, too, will fall under the control of the Hilruda."

Zerek took a minute to think about that. "You're trying to unite the clans. To go to war."

"Speaking of war is... premature. But yes."

"What the fuck took you so long? The Hilruda have been encroaching on your territory for years. Why wait until now?"

Essian's expression was even more inscrutable, or perhaps he was just harder to read in profile. "My father was one of many who believe uniting the clans will only end in disaster, like when the seers were destroyed."

"That's the reason for all the secrecy. Your father wasn't the only one who was against trying to unite the clans."

"My sources told me you were intelligent. I'm glad to see that proven. Yes, I fear the possibility of someone trying something drastic to stop me. But I'm clan leader now, and I don't think we can wait any longer. Otherwise, there will be no clan for the children to inherit."

Zerek agreed. He didn't give a fluffy fuck what some long dead seer thought about the matter. None of the clans on their own could stand against the concerted efforts of the Hilruda, and it would only be a matter of time before they moved against the Kadrussians in earnest. For the chance to foul up the Hilruda's plans, Zerek would have agreed to do this job for free, despite the increase in danger. But then, people didn't generally trust free, which meant Zerek didn't feel any burning need to renegotiate their agreed upon terms.

"I'm sorry for the loss of your father." Zerek hadn't sensed any real grief, but clan leaders probably weren't allowed that luxury.

"Thank you. We didn't have a lot of common ground, but he was still my father."

That might have been the most personal thing Essian had said. In case it pained Essian, Zerek turned the conversation to less emotionally charged topics.

Zerek finished setting up their meager camp. Essian—or his people—had done a good job of estimating what equipment and supplies they'd need. Only a few adjustments and additions had been necessary, but when their only source of transport was their own two feet, sacrifices had to be made. This camp was probably the roughest he'd had to endure in years, but the location more than made up for it.

Prime, prime location. Plenty of greenery for shelter and cover. Wild berries and edible roots abounded, to round out their tasteless, but nutritional staples. A nearby creek for water and bathing. Zerek was getting spoiled in his old age of twenty-nine. These days, he much preferred to be clean, especially when in the company of an attractive man. The heat of the day and Zerek's increased attraction to Essian made him sweat far more than he'd like. Walking in the daylight heated Essian up too, but only to the point of making his spicy scent more noticeable, and more than once, Zerek caught himself inhaling deeply trying to catch a whiff. Essian wasn't cursed with unpleasant body odor—maybe Kadrussians didn't do that.

Several times, Essian's partially split tongue flickered out. Maybe Essian was scenting for threats. Or, maybe it was a body cooling mechanism. Either option was more palatable than checking for Zerek's stink.

"You want to bathe first or second?" Zerek had no problem interpreting the questioning look. "It's one of the reasons I chose this place to stay for the night. We can take turns washing up in the creek."

Zerek half expected him to ask why they'd take turns, but Essian wasn't stupid. He had to know that it was safer if one of them stood guard. Not that Zerek expected trouble this soon, but better to be over vigilant than to get dead or recaptured.

"I will go first."

Stupid to give Essian a choice. Zerek should have gone first, because he had no doubt watching Essian get naked and bathe was only going to make it doubly embarrassing when it came to his turn.

Then again, getting turned on was inevitable, and he'd pretty much resigned himself to several days of traveling while semi-aroused.

Guard duty tested Zerek's self-control like nothing else. Essian was exactly the type of guy he preferred, and rarely found. Zerek was a big, muscular guy—stronger than most other men he came across. Kadrussians were a bigger, stronger species, and Essian was an elite specimen. His distinct color pattern extended over his whole body, as Zerek discovered from several hopefully surreptitious peeks, including one that gave him a glimpse of a mouth-watering cock. The gold overtones were simply stunning when he moved into the sunlight.

Sinuously, Essian slid into the water, and helplessly, Zerek watched, mesmerized by the water sheeting off that tempting skin, large hands stroking over firm muscles. Cock throbbing mercilessly in his pants, Zerek forced himself to turn away and check the surroundings for any threats. The Serpentes clan would make sure his death was drawn out and painful if he'd let their leader get hurt because he'd been beguiled by Essian's nudity.

After an eternity, Essian arose from the creek. Zerek waited for a moment, but Essian made no move to get dressed.

"What are you waiting for, Zerek?"

So many answers to that question, and not one of them appropriate. "Aren't you getting dressed?"

"No. I prefer to dry before I put my clothes back on. You go ahead though. It will not affect my ability to stand guard."

Sweet mother's milk. Never mind irate clan members, Essian was going to kill him dead right here. If unfulfilled desire didn't get him, Essian might do the job if he realized how turned on Zerek was.

Stepping out of Essian's direct line of sight, he started to strip. Although he kept an eye out, Essian never turned to check out Zerek's bared body. Flaring of Essian's longer, narrower, nostrils were the only sign that he wasn't a lifeless statue. Zerek didn't recall ever seeing a Kadrussian do it before—the slightly different nasal structure made it quite obvious—and had no idea what would cause such a reaction.

Cold water and Essian's painful disinterest quieted his cock, however temporarily, but didn't do a thing to wash away the disappointment. Foolish of him to care, especially when he couldn't quite pinpoint why Essian fascinated him so much.

Dwelling on the rejection wasn't in anyone's best interest, and he floundered for a topic change. "I don't know much about clan leadership. Are you the oldest of your father's children?"

Muscles twitched in Essian's back, and masochistically, Zerek dropped his gaze to a spectacular, gleaming ass. When his cock threatened to come to life, despite the chilled water, he raised his eyes again. Essian hadn't answered and he cleared his throat, wondering if he needed to speak up.

"I am my father's only child."

"Oh. So..." Zerek couldn't think of a good way to say it, but he wanted to know. "I don't want to sound pessimistic, but what if something happens to you?"

For the first time, Essian's hissed laughter had a distinctly unhappy tinge. "I have children to secure the clan leadership."

Children. When he'd spoken of children to inherit the clan, Zerek hadn't realized he was talking about his own kids. Disappointment welled up, hot and choking. Of course Essian wouldn't be attracted to another man.

"You left one of them in charge?"

This time, Essian snorted. "No. My council of elders will oversee clan business until my return. None of my children have reached maturity, and even so, my eldest shows no signs of being fit to rule. The next, though, she shows promise."

"What do you mean, fit to rule? Competitors aren't exiled or killed are they?" Zerek had visions of a Kadrussian version of the Stony Gate pit fights, but to the death.

Essian whipped around, golden eyes narrowed. "Are you suggesting I killed off my siblings?" His words held more hissing than normal, presumably due to fangs that had lengthened to a more threatening size.

Zerek held up his hands in what he hoped was an unthreatening manner, but resolutely refused to step back. Last thing he wanted was to get bitten—Essian's venom would undoubtedly be lethal—but he'd faced danger many times before. "Sorry. I just...don't know how it works."

With an agitated tongue flicker, Essian spun around and Zerek pursed his lips. He'd had a chance to check out a fully naked Essian from the front, and fear of Essian's anger meant he'd missed it. Of all the mud sucking luck.

The creek burbled happily, while Zerek waited for Essian to say something.

"I am sorry too. I shouldn't have gotten angry over an innocent question. I meant that my son doesn't have the temperament or desire to lead. Forcing him into that role will only make everyone unhappy. Siblings, if they exist, often become part of the circle of clan leader's advisors. Leadership does not always fall to the eldest."

"Two kids, that's a good number." Like Zerek knew. In the encampments, more kids meant more hands to help with work, but meant more mouths to feed as well. He had no idea what a good number was for anyone, much less a clan leader.

"I have eight children. Another way in which I differed from my father. He was barely fertile."

Aside from knowing Essian had a whole litter of kids and proved fertile, there was something odd about his words, but Zerek sensed pushing wouldn't get him anything.

He also wanted to know if the mother of his children was a true mate he'd heard stories about. Like the prophecy and the seers, Zerek didn't believe in the concept of a true mate, but he knew the Kadrussians did. Marriages and procreation happened in their absence, though, so Zerek assumed the concept was some sort of delusion on the part of love-sick people.

Imagining Essian with his true mate was like having hundreds of splinters in his skin, so he turned his thoughts toward the challenges of the following day while he finished washing. Tomorrow, they'd face the first place where Zerek's skills would truly be useful.

Unlike Essian, he pulled on his underclothes while he was still damp. Past experience taught him they'd dry quickly enough, and he needed something to hide behind. Being naked with a man he desired, who didn't desire him back, made him feel more vulnerable than anything else in his life.

CHAPTER FOUR

Zerek paid careful attention to the lay of the land. They hadn't quite left Serpentes territory, but less than an hour's journey would put them in the communal passage, the buffer zone between clan territories and Hilruda controlled land. Ostensibly, it had been created long before humans arrived to provide a neutral area to avoid conflict between the two species, but in reality, it ended up a lawless length of land that had, until recently, been a refuge of human escapees.

With the border Kadrussian clans slowly pulling back closer to the clan heartlands, the Hilruda had "altruistically" taken it upon themselves to police the communal passage. Effectively, that meant the communal passage was no longer neutral, but under Hilruda control. People who took it upon themselves to try and escape the Hilruda now faced getting picked up by a Hilruda patrol and likely finding themselves in Stony Gate, or traveling deep into clan territory and risk running into unfriendly Kadrussians.

Zerek couldn't blame the Kadrussians for reacting badly to border incursions. Flooding the clan lands with destitute and desperate humans wouldn't solve the Hilruda problem at all, which is why Zerek tried to be discerning when he brokered a smuggling deal for human passage and permanent living arrangements in the clan lands. Although it wouldn't be long before he had to come up with another solution.

Coming to a halt, he grabbed Essian's arm.

"Is something wrong?"

"No, but we're almost at the crossroads market and we need to get ready." Zerek slung the pack off his back and dug inside for one of the hooded cloaks like the ones his Kadrussian rescuers had worn to get him out of Stony Gate. He showed it to Essian. "Get yours out."

Essian obeyed, but he wasn't happy. "The crossroads market? What are we doing here? There is a more direct route to Philae clan lands, and we don't risk getting caught by the Hilruda."

"You did specifically want my help, right? Because I have reasons for everything I do." Not all of which had to do with Essian's travel plans, but Zerek's agenda and Essian's did overlap in this case. A slight detour was called for.

Essian compressed his lips together before wrapping himself in the hooded cloak. Zerek followed suit, then assessed his companion critically.

"The second we leave the tree line, I want you to slouch."

"Slouch?" Essian said it like it was a dirty word and Zerek shook his head. Probably the Serpentes clan leader didn't have to hide himself often. Or ever.

"Yes, slouch. Like this." Zerek demonstrated, folding in on himself. He had more practice than Essian did, but after a few moments, Essian had compressed himself in a commendable manner.

"Why exactly am I doing this?"

"Because we're both bigger than most humans. We don't want to draw any unnecessary attention while we're at the market. Even though the market stands on traditionally neutral lands, the Hilruda still patrol, and Kadrussian attendees are few. If we can convince casual observers we're nothing more than normal humans, we'll be better off." Zerek didn't know if it was possible to remain undetected, but attending the market was a risk he needed to take.

"If we are missing supplies, why didn't you say that before we left my stronghold?"

Essian was too damned straightforward for smuggling, and he asked a lot of questions. Most times when Zerek was smuggling people out of Hilruda territory, they were too desperate and defeated to do anything but do what he said.

"Look. Can you just trust me, Mister Mysterious Prophecy? Don't think I haven't noticed you haven't told me everything yet. But I'm trusting you to tell me what I need to know. You need to slouch and don't speak unless you have to. No constantly questioning my actions until after we're clear of the market, got it?"

A tiny hiss was the only obvious sign of Essian's displeasure, but he nodded sharply.

They turned from their original direction to head for the communal passage. He'd rather come out on the passage far from potential observers. Easier to pretend they'd been traveling from Hilruda territory, rather than popping out of clan territory. Even so, once they were out of the thick brush, the muted noise of a large group of people was audible and the cacophony of the market increased with every step.

"Follow me closely," Zerek whispered to Essian as they reached the outskirts.

The goods at market were rarely luxurious or well crafted—most of those were appropriated by the Hilruda—but Zerek made a point of stopping at seemingly random stalls. More to the point, he wanted to look like he was innocently browsing, but certain stalls had vendors who were more entrenched with their Hilruda masters than Zerek thought wise, for anyone's sake. He also didn't want anyone to take note of the one vendor he needed to talk to, the whole reason he'd made straight for the crossroads market.

Essian shifted impatiently each time Zerek stopped at a stall, and grumbled when he exchanged a few copper beads for useless ribbons and candy. Despite the Hilruda oppression, courting rituals had never disappeared from the human instinct. Ribbons and candy from the market were the most common items for a man to bring his sweetheart.

After wending through half the market, there didn't seem to be anyone taking special notice of them, and Zerek casually approached his goal, the vendor from which he'd bought his bone lock picks.

"Hello, good sir." Arri's patter was well practiced. "Can I interest you in some finely crafted bone tools? Or utensils?"

"Have you any oteryan combs?" Oteryan, though an attractively plumed avian, had bones far too porous to work into anything more useful than airy, decorative pieces that no human could reasonably afford. Definitely wouldn't be used for anything functional. A subtle jolt swept Arri's frame, but was quickly suppressed. Zerek smiled under his hood. No reason for Arri to have forgotten their signal, even if it had been months since he'd last sought out information from the crossroads market.

"I have something that might just suit your purpose." Arri made a show of pulling out a series of decorative combs that anyone should be able to tell weren't oteryan bone, but like any good salesman, outright telling a customer he was a fool wasn't good business. Essian moved on to inspect the goods at a stall farther along, and Zerek took advantage of his distraction to ask the questions he wanted. Pretty soon, though, Zerek had to get Essian out of the market before his impatience drew negative attention.

"Any news from The City?" The Hilruda had more than one, but only one contained Stony Gate, the same one that housed the Hilruda governing body. Any of the smaller ones were referred to by name, but only one was The City. For a long time, he'd wondered why the ultimate masters of the Hilruda resided in the same city as the enormous prison, but they probably got the biggest share of the energy from the pit fights. With some effort, Zerek curtailed a shudder.

"Indeed. Big escape from Stony Gate. The masters were, are unbelievably furious." Arri's voice had dropped and he glanced around.

32

Even if Arri hadn't been part of his network, talking about something that pissed off the Hilruda wasn't wise.

"Oh? You don't say."

"Yep. Famous smuggler. Being hailed as a hero by many... when the masters aren't around."

Fuck. Hero? He was no hero, and it wasn't even an escape by his own means. But correcting Arri would not be wise. The less Arri knew, the better.

"Famous smuggler?"

"Zerek, ever heard of him?" Arri had cultivated the persona of a gossip, which meant Zerek could get information out in the open without anyone getting suspicious.

"Yes, perhaps. Didn't he have a crew? Did they escape too?" Long practice in his chosen vocation was the only thing that kept his voice steady and casual as he asked that question. Zerek glanced at Essian, but he was still a couple stalls away. Not that he didn't believe Essian, but he needed confirmation from his own people.

"Nah, they're still on the loose, although word is they've gone to ground to let tempers cool."

Zerek closed his eyes and let out a breath. One less thing to worry about it, and it had been a major concern from the moment he'd been imprisoned.

"My favorite theory about the escape was that Zerek was spirited away by ghosts." Arri chuckled. "Another popular one is that yo... uh... he's a shapeshifter."

Arri mentioned a couple more outlandish theories about how Zerek had escaped while Zerek touched a few of the combs on display. Fortunately, no mention was made of the Kadrussians, which was another minor worry off his mind. At an appropriate point, Zerek wedged in another question, his air of boredom not entirely feigned.

"Heard anything about passage to the northern wilds?" The wilds spanned both sides of Hilruda and Kadrussian lands, and once past the wilds on the one side was the last clan Zerek and Essian intended to visit.

"The northern wilds?" Arri looked thoughtful. "Probably avoid the Tyran valley. And maybe the Grathern Forest. I heard the patrols were...vigorous in taking down a couple of tent cities. I understand they're lingering to make sure they've rounded everyone up."

"Good to know. I'll take this comb here." Zerek paid Arri in copper beads, using a practiced bit of sleight of hand to pass over far more than the asking price of the comb. Arri wrapped the comb and Zerek tucked the package into his pack.

He paused at a couple more stalls before leading an increasingly agitated Essian out of the market. Amazingly, the man waited until they were well into the trees before he ripped off his hood.

"What did that prove? Candy? Ribbons? Combs? That was a waste of time and copper beads, the same ones you insisted be included in your pack."

"Oh, for fuck's sake. The Kadrussians are swimming in copper—it hardly ruined you." Copper was one of the few metals humans were allowed to possess, which made it a convenient currency. "Aside from that, my purpose was hardly shopping. It's not like I have a desperate need for candy."

"Then what was that? The northern wilds? We're heading to Philae now, not Tilia."

This was the most emotional he'd seen Essian, and it was both sexy and amusing, watching him huff and hiss, kicking at the dirt. Perverse bastard that he was, he enjoyed thwarting Essian's expectations. Probably weren't too many in Essian's life who did that, and Zerek had too many years of experience doing it to the Hilruda to turn it off that easily. Even if he wanted to. Which he didn't, because Essian needed to learn a lesson about eavesdropping. Thankfully, Hilruda hearing wasn't nearly as acute as a Kadrussian's, which Zerek hadn't realized until now.

"*That* is called information gathering. If anyone was actually listening to that conversation, or if Arri is interrogated, he can tell them where I said I was going. Since we're planning to visit Tilia last, our path is going to be quite a bit different than it would be if we were setting off from here. That means a better chance of evading anyone looking for us. Or rather, me."

Essian flickered his tongue out as he stared at Zerek. A few moments later, the angry tension dissolved.

"Good idea. Perhaps you should have overpaid for the comb."

Zerek chuckled. Probably as close to an apology he was going to get. "I did overpay him, but you missed it, so likely others did as well."

Essian looked suitably impressed. At least Zerek was able to do something right for this important client.

"What are tent cities?"

"Sometimes humans will congregate in areas that they think are safe and away from the Hilruda. Gradually, word gets around, and the numbers swell. At a certain size, it's almost impossible to keep it secret. Like trying to keep a whole village secret. The Hilruda patrols will sweep in and capture everyone. Some go to Stony Gate, but most are pressed back into service, often the more dismal and degrading tasks."

"But the Grathern Forest isn't in Hilruda territory. Neither is most of the Tyran valley."

Zerek nodded. "I know, but no Kadrussians live there, nor do they patrol often. Humans think it's safe because no one's there and the Hilruda know there won't be any repercussions for excursions into your territory."

The information did not please Essian. "I knew it was bad, but I hadn't realized just how bad."

Wasn't that the truth? Bad enough for Zerek's people to have two concurrent tent cities big enough to catch interest, and bad that the Hilruda had no compunction about venturing so far past the communal passage.

"Then we'd better get a move on. You've got a prophecy to fulfill, and the sooner we're done, the sooner I can go back to helping my people. We're not going to make the Philae stronghold before nightfall, and I want to set up camp as far from the market as possible."

Without another word, Essian allowed Zerek to head out. They walked in silence for a couple of hours before Essian spoke again.

"I had told you your crew was safe. Did you not believe me?" The tone was soft, without a hint of rancor or arrogance.

"Essian, you've got advisors, and friends, and children." For some reason, Zerek didn't want to mention the obvious—a wife. No matter how useless to even entertain the idea that they might *entertain* each other during their journey. "You don't know what it's like to be alone. But my crew, they saved my sanity. I handpicked them for their skills and they became friends. Family. Or at least the closest I'll ever have. I needed answers from someone I've known more than a few days. Can you understand that?"

Essian nodded. "Of course. Forgive me."

Zerek shrugged. "Now, if you don't mind, we ought to be quiet for a while. We're still too close to the market for comfort."

And he didn't want to talk anymore. For some reason, he'd revealed a very personal thing to a near stranger, which wasn't like him. He just hoped his gut was telling him the truth about Essian, and that he wasn't going to regret showing Essian any of his vulnerabilities.

Around a bend in the road, the Phinae stronghold appeared. Trepidation knotted his guts, tempering Zerek's good mood. First thing that morning, they'd by-passed a Hilruda scouting party and nosy Kadrussians with relative ease.

A couple times since they'd left the market, Zerek found himself smiling as he remembered the ridiculous explanations Arri had heard about his miraculous escape from Stony Gate. Not knowing the answer must be whipping the Hilruda into frothing fury. Considering he was still feeling the ill effects of his single fight at Stony Gate, it was no more than they deserved, may their festering balls rot and fall off.

They'd made good time to the stronghold, but it had been an arduous trip. Much to his annoyance, Essian had more stamina than he did, and Zerek continued to push himself harder than normal in an effort to impress the reserved Essian. Even in top form, he'd be hard pressed to match the Kadrussian's athleticism.

In minutes, they stood before a heavy, wooden door, the only way through a substantial stone barrier. The upper levels of the stronghold were visible above the wall, more resembling a rocky outcropping of the mountain than a building. Tired and disheveled, Zerek took in the number of guards he could see. There were probably more he couldn't. If Essian was wrong about getting in to see the clan leader, they would be dead in seconds. He should have fucking pressed Essian for details. He blamed his stupidity on the Hilruda trying to eat him and his cock for appropriating more than its fair share of blood.

Both of them remained hidden under cloaks, and Zerek drew his closer about him. No matter that humans resided in clan lands, there weren't enough that his humanness would go unnoticed and unremarked. Flaunting it wouldn't be wise.

Essian approached the guards, Zerek following closely enough to help if things went badly. Few Kadrussians bothered with weapons, but Zerek had insisted on taking at least a couple of knives with him. Not like he had poisonous fangs to rely on. Even in simple strength, Zerek would be hard pressed to hold his own with many clansmen. The guards, though, carried spears tipped with sharp points that appeared far more functional than ceremonial.

"Your purpose?" The guard that spoke was a muscular woman, not nearly as big as Essian or the other guards, but that didn't make her any less dangerous.

"I am a Seeker on a true mate quest."

Zerek's eyes widened. What the fuck was going on? Nevertheless, a ripple of excitement seemed to emanate from those who heard Essian's words. Essian stepped back, and they waited.

Questions bubbled up in his throat, and only the fact that the guards were still observing them kept them locked behind his teeth.

In surprisingly short order, a man whose bearing resembled Essian's bodyguard took charge of them as he led them through the stronghold.

He stopped at a guest suite and opened the door. "You may rest and refresh here. Someone will come to fetch you for your audience with the clan leader. Are you both Seekers?"

Essian shook his head. "No. My companion serves as guide. The paths between our lands grow treacherous."

"Indeed. The Hilruda dogs have become bold."

Zerek didn't know if that meant the guard would be in favor of Essian's plan to unite the clans against the Hilruda, but then, it wasn't the guard they were here to see. Of course, he didn't know everything that was going on. Zerek may have heard of true mates, but he didn't know what a true mate quest or a seeker was, and he was furious that Essian had decided on this subterfuge without preparing him. Assuming he hadn't been lying his ass off to Zerek the whole fucking time about the purpose of this journey.

The second they were alone, Zerek slung his pack into the corner, yanked off his hooded cloak, and turned on Essian. "What is going on? We had hours of traveling. At some point you could have shared something. How does this help?"

Zerek should probably be gratified by Essian's apologetic expression, but he wasn't. He didn't even feel one bit of remorse for yelling at a clan leader.

Essian gestured for Zerek to quiet down.

He drew in breath to get even louder when he felt it. The prickle of eyes on him. Or if not eyes, then ears. He might have been taken by surprise, and be somewhat out of his element, but there was a reason he'd never been caught. Without someone betraying him, anyway.

Instead, he stalked over to a table with food and drink. So very similar to his experience in Essian's territory, he could almost imagine that they'd walked for days and ended up in the same place.

Essian joined him, and the food was almost gone before the Kadrussian clan leader looked at him.

"You're probably not familiar with a true mate quest."

"You would be right." Zerek didn't even try to keep his tone from conveying his disgruntlement.

"And true mates?"

Zerek waved a hand. "Fated lovers, or spouses, or something." Sounded like bedtime stories his grandfather told him when he was a kid. Most of his grandfather's stories revolved around the time before the Bitter Silence, stories that were forbidden by the Hilruda, but his grandfather had been a biologist before such professions were outlawed. He'd been fascinated by the different species sharing the planet.

"I won't try to convince you about the truth of the matter, but true mates are revered. Not everyone finds theirs, and some don't care if they find them. But a true mate quest is sacred among our people."

"I still don't know..." Zerek glanced around the room. It wouldn't take long for people to figure out he was human, which meant this explanation could be innocent enough for anyone listening in. Anything he didn't infer from what Essian couldn't say, well, Zerek would beat it out of him on the way to the next clan.

"Although it's largely ceremonial, all Seekers are granted an audience with the clan leader. A gathering of suitable mates will be organized in fairly short order, and if I am deemed worthy, the group will include candidates from the clan leader's family. A true mate quest is the cause for much festivity."

Great. He was smuggling Essian across half of Kadrussian territory so he could go to fancy parties. And attempt to find a "true mate." The only thing that kept him from flipping the table upside down and leaving Essian here to fend for himself was that Essian would be meeting with the clan leader. He wasn't telling Zerek everything, that was for sure, but there had to be a point in this ceremony where Essian believed he'd have enough time alone with the clan leader to discuss plans for uniting against the Hilruda.

Essian leaned across the table, and Zerek got a noseful of his spicy, masculine scent, somehow smelling more intoxicating despite their physical exertion since bathing in the creek. Despite the impossibility of the situation, he instantly hardened. Logic didn't matter to his cock.

"You must always refer to me as Seeker." The pupils of Essian's eyes flared as his tongue snaked out briefly.

Zerek shifted in his seat, trying to hide his erection. "Why?"

"True mates are equals. Identity, rank, and status should be immaterial, and shouldn't affect one's decision to accept the bond."

Huh. Zerek actually liked the way that sounded. "Then why are some candidates held back?" He'd pump Essian later about how "worthiness" was determined.

Essian laughed, his happy one. "It wouldn't be much a quest if there were no obstacles, would it?"

Cultural differences—sometimes they were simply incomprehensible.

"We'd better get bathing, if we're going to be ready." Figures no one gave them a precise time.

But Essian shook his head. "I will bathe first. But you will have to remain here."

"No. Unacceptable. You can't leave me here like an unwanted pet."

"A human has yet to observe a true mate quest. To allow one would make this journey more gossip worthy than it already is."

Gossip. Fuck. He'd known the Kadrussians he'd seen in the stronghold had been vibrating with excitement.

"If there's gossip, how do you expect to remain anonymous?"

"It is a matter of honor. It doesn't matter if you know the identity of the Seeker. We are honor bound not to discuss it until the quest has been completed."

"Fine. I can use an early night in a proper bed."

Essian stood, but before he went to bathe, he leaned down, lips close enough to kiss his ear. "All clan leaders will know me by sight. They will comply with my request to talk alone, and respect the need for secrecy."

The warmth of Essian's breath tickling his neck made his cock fully harden with almost painful swiftness. Breathing deeply, he waited until Essian closed the door to the bathing room, then he groaned and dropped his head. Somehow he was going to have to hide how attracted he found Essian for days and days. This was only the first of five stops, and if they didn't encounter any problems, that meant at least three weeks together, but more like three and a half. Torture. Or humiliation. No, both, which was even worse.

Zerek made a show of taking his pack apart and meticulously repacking it to give him something to do, but that didn't stop him from imagining Essian in the water. All he had to do was call to mind that afternoon in the creek. He knew how incredible Essian looked naked and wet. All he was doing was making his cock harder.

Essian banged out of the bathing room, startling Zerek and making him hunch over the pack.

Out of the corner of his eye, he saw Essian's tongue flicker out, but Essian was fully dressed again. Too bad.

"What are you doing?"

"Just repacking the bag. See if I can tighten it up any."

Essian gave a little hiss of agreement? Praise? Zerek had to figure out more of the Kadrussian non-verbal cues.

The door swung in with a bang. A slender Kadrussian man entered carrying a large tray, which he placed on the table and retreated without a word.

"Good. Here's some food for you."

"For me? That's a lot of food for me. Aren't you eating?"

"There will be food at the ceremony. Don't wait up for me. It could be late before I return."

Zerek blinked, and Essian was gone, leaving a swirl of spicy scent and the echoing bang of the door slamming shut. Stunned, he stood there for a few moments, mouth hanging open. Fuck that. He wasn't getting left behind.

He sprinted to the door, intending to follow Essian, regardless.

"Fuck, fuck, fuck." The door was locked. Locked! They were serious about him not observing the ceremony.

Slumping down on a chair by the table, he considered his options. There weren't any windows for him to escape out of, since the entire stronghold had been built into the side of a mountain. He could make a ruckus, try to break out, or he could be the good little untrusted paid help.

He lifted a cover on the tray and sniffed. At least he'd be well-fed paid help. First, though, a bath.

Minutes later, he was sliding into heated water. Such a luxury. As he was soaping himself up, he suddenly realized he was alone. All alone in the suite, and unlikely to be disturbed because of Essian's private ceremony. His hands began to caress more than they cleaned, and his cock didn't need much coaxing to revive.

The soap slicked him perfectly, and he started up a lazy stroke from base to head. Only the tip of his plump cock broke the surface of the water, his arm's movement creating ripples.

He paused for a moment, wondering if he was maybe being observed, but then decided he didn't care. It had been too fucking long since he'd had any release and anyone observing the bathing room had to expect to get an eyeful of cock. Another stroke of his erection and his brief concern faded.

Would Essian touch him gently, or rough? What about that tongue? Zerek's cock jumped in his hand, and he squeezed it just a little harder. That tongue would probably feel amazing sliding up his cock, flickering around the head, moving lower.

Zerek cupped his balls with his other hand, massaging gently. Didn't feel like a tongue at all, but the touch sent him deeper into the fantasy.

Maybe Essian would even lick further down. Not many men had licked his hole, but it would be a shame to waste that agile tongue on nothing more than cock sucking.

It would open him up, provide some initial slickness. Zerek rubbed a finger over his hole while he stroked his cock, firm and tight.

With a guttural groan, he shot into the air, each pulse landing with a tiny splash in the water. Before the cum could separate and get gross, he swept it up in a washcloth and flung it on the floor.

Sated, relaxed, and clean he sank down into the tub, but when his eyes fluttered closed he pushed himself up. This trip would be immeasurably more humiliating if Essian returned to find him sleeping naked in icy bath water. Assuming he didn't just drown.

Hoisting himself out of the bath was tricky, as his muscles were twitchy. It had been a fine orgasm for one self-induced, but it shouldn't wipe him out like this. Not even after his days of constant hiking.

Fucking turd juggling Hilruda. How long was it going to take before he recovered?

He dragged on a clean pair of pants and looked sadly at the spread of food. Never mind breaking out of here and chasing down Essian, he didn't have enough energy to do the food justice. He grabbed a thick hunk of bread and chewed on it before trudging to the nearest door that led to a bed chamber. At least he didn't have to share a bed with Essian. Keeping his hands to himself under those circumstances might be impossible.

Snuggling under the covers, he had to admit that considering the circumstances, this wasn't so bad. Sure, he was pissed at being left behind like an unruly pet, and his curiosity was champing to observe the super-secret ceremony, but having some alone time to deal with the urges Essian elicited wasn't the worst thing. Nor was getting to sleep early in a comfortable bed. For now, he'd play nice. And whether or not Essian was truly on one of these mate quests, the idea made a decent subterfuge.

All hail sacred tradition.

CHAPTER FIVE

By late afternoon the next day, they were hours away from the Philae stronghold, heading for the next clan lands. He'd slept so soundly he had no idea when Essian returned to the suite, but Essian had been in the other bedroom, asleep, when Zerek awoke and finished off the remains of dinner. If not for the food and sleep, Zerek could only imagine how much worse he'd feel. It was like he'd aged five or ten years. His general listlessness wasn't debilitating, it just wasn't normal. All he could hope for was that he would recover, the sooner the better, may all Hilruda rot into oily slime.

Since they'd left the Philae stronghold, they'd not said one word to each other. By nature and practice, Zerek was reticent, but this was ridiculous. His voice might malfunction entirely if he didn't use it more than this. And Zerek's mind was dipping far too often into sexual fantasies, which made hiking that much more uncomfortable.

He wanted to ask if Essian had gotten the cooperation or agreement he needed from the Philae clan leader, but he suspected that information might be considered confidential. Part of him wanted to ask if Essian had found his true mate, but mostly he wasn't sure he wanted to know that. There was also a part of him that was still a little annoyed about being left behind and locked in, despite the fact he'd managed to get a good night's sleep.

Sulking didn't become him, but he also wasn't sure how to open the lines of communication. After all, they'd already spent the better part of a week together without doing more than snatches of small talk in between long stretches of silence. He wasn't sure if he could handle a whole month of it.

"You told me earlier that your crew was your family. How is it you don't have any other family?" The sudden explosion of words in the silence was almost startling, but Essian's tone was sympathetic.

Zerek wanted to kiss Essian for saying something, anything. Okay, so he wanted to do that anyway, even if it meant navigating those fangs, but he had to consider the question. After all, his rule of thumb was always to keep his personal stuff personal so it couldn't be used against him. Then again, his gut told him Essian wouldn't do that, and Zerek's head couldn't find any logical reason Essian would want to.

"My parents died when I was a baby. The Hilruda force their servants to live and work under atrocious conditions, and sickness spreads quickly. One such infection was quite deadly, and according to my grandfather, seemed to target healthy adults more than it did the elderly, infants, and the infirm. My grandfather raised me until he died, and then I was on my own."

"How old were you?"

"Twelve."

"Twelve? You've been on your own since you were twelve? Why?"

Zerek shrugged. "My grandfather was the last of my family, and no one else had time or food to spare for an orphan boy. I made do by stealing and surviving off garbage. I had two goals—find enough food to survive and avoid running afoul of the Hilruda."

"I'm surprised the Hilruda didn't put you to work. They would have considered you fit enough at twelve to do a number of tasks."

Zerek grimaced slightly. At least Essian hadn't sounded as if he agreed with those shit-squelchers, that kids of twelve should be put to work, especially under the "optimal" conditions the Hilruda developed.

"Let's just say I come by my hatred of the Hilruda honestly. My grandfather remembered the time before the Bitter Silence. He'd tell me stories about it, when no one was around to hear and turn him in. He didn't want me to live and die like my parents, and when he sickened, he helped me prepare for a life on my own. A lot of it I had to learn on my own, but I was motivated."

He told a couple of stories about childish pranks he'd played on the Hilruda, Essian rewarding him with that hissing laugh of his. Better to tell the good stories than the ones where he hadn't been sure he'd survive.

"So how did you get into smuggling?"

"I started out stealing food, but soon graduated to more valuable items. Smuggling seemed a natural progression, and I started developing contacts all over, including a few Kadrussians in the border clans."

During which, he created his crew, eventually becoming his own little ramshackle family.

"Smuggling people into the clan lands was a natural progression?" Essian's doubt was probably justified, and Zerek laughed.

"Okay, maybe not. But after a while, just being a thorny problem for the Hilruda wasn't enough. I wanted to do something more significant. Remember, I was raised on stories of the human condition before the Bitter

Silence. Right about when I was looking for a new purpose in life, I chanced upon one of the masters whipping a pregnant servant girl. She was my first relocation, and suddenly I had new goals and aspirations."

Essian let out a purr which made Zerek feel content, but he didn't know why. Still, he'd talked more about himself than he'd ever done with anyone.

"What was it like growing up the son of a clan leader? The heir?"

This time, Essian's hiss was decidedly less jovial. "Lonely. My father was quite old when he finally sired me. He'd been trying for decades to continue the line."

Right, Zerek remembered the uncomfortable discussion about *fertility*. "Surely you didn't need siblings to not be lonely."

"No, but my father kept me quite isolated. He was worried if I played with other children I'd get hurt and die. Or suffer some childhood disease. I even had tutors so I didn't need to attend school like everyone else. I spent my childhood in the company of my father's advisors, learning only how to rule a clan."

"Wow. Even when I was running wild as a kid, I still had time for fun. I'm sorry."

Essian turned, his lips stretched in a smile wide enough to bare both fangs. "I, too, became something of an escape artist when I was young. Not good enough to be professional, though."

Zerek laughed. "Well, I guess we have something in common."

"I guess we do."

An odd silence enveloped them, and Zerek pulled Essian to a halt, gesturing for him to remain silent. He listened closely, but the normal forest fauna had ceased their normal activity. Pulling his knife out, he brandished it in front of him while he peered into the underbrush surrounding them.

A faint rustle had him facing east, then he heard a distinctive rattle.

"Climb a tree. Now." He whirled around. East was the only safe direction right now, and he hoped Essian had enough sense to follow his orders.

Seconds later, a quelar burst out of the brush, horned head lowered as it charged. Zerek braced himself. There were only so many places a knife could slip through their roughened reptilian hide. His knife was long enough to extend his reach, and the quelar was fairly small. As long as he could avoid getting gored, he had a chance.

At the very last second, he leapt out of the way while jabbing the knife down, trying to get the base of the creature's skull. The impact jarred his shoulder painfully, but despite a brief numbness, he managed to hold onto the knife. He turned around to prepare for another charge, when Essian jumped on the back of the beast, bearing it to the ground with his larger bulk. This time, his fangs were longer and more pronounced as he sank them in the shoulder of the quelar. The reptile rattled and grunted, but quickly succumbed to the Kadrussian venom.

Essian stood slowly, wiping his mouth. Too bad they were so far from the crossroads market. Arri would pay a hefty sum for a quelar he didn't have to hunt himself.

"That was very brave of you."

Zerek frowned. "What do you mean?"

"I can protect myself. You didn't need to take the quelar on by yourself. But thank you for your quick thinking."

Yes, of course. Risk the Serpentes clan leader getting gored by a quelar. That wouldn't do his reputation any good. Never mind his own personal reasons for ensuring Essian didn't get hurt.

"Have you hunted quelar before? I thought your father had been over protective."

"No, I haven't hunted quelar before. I've been instructed in the theory. But make no mistake, I can still fight. My father was over protective of me as a child, but once I matured, I switched my tutors for fight instructors. A clan leader must be able to protect himself."

"Oh. Thanks for the assistance."

"I'm sure you didn't need it." Essian's words could have been condescending, but they weren't. Not at all. "I must admit, when I was told they had the capability to create sounds in a direction different from where they approach, I hadn't believed it. Quite remarkable."

"Yeah. My grandfather used to say they "threw their voice". I don't know where he came up with that term, because they don't have a voice, really. The noise you really need to listen for is the rattle." Zerek nudged the tail, resulting in muted rattle. "That's what gives away their position, not the false call to herd frightened animals closer to them."

Actually, the incident turned out well for them. They could leave the carcass to be picked clean by other animals in the area instead of hiding it. If a Hilruda patrol came across the dead quelar, a Kadrussian killing bite wouldn't be nearly as suspicious as a knife wound.

The adrenaline pumped Zerek up a bit, and for the next hour or so, he felt like his old self as they continued on their journey.

"Essian, I have contacts with the border clans, but I was wondering if, when all this is over, if I could get you to introduce me to some of the interior clans. Or maybe have some of your people do so. I don't necessarily need to talk to anyone at the clan leader or advisor level."

The idea had been stewing in his mind since he heard about the tent cities, and he hoped the successful altercation with the quelar would put Essian in an amenable mood.

"Why?"

"There are always more humans who need to escape. The journey would be longer, but entering into agreements with more clans would provide good homes for the most mistreated of my people to settle. It's not just charity. They can all contribute to daily life."

Essian hissed, but the soft one that Zerek thought meant approval. "I will arrange it as soon as I return to my clan."

Zerek breathed out a sigh of relief. Sexy, kind, and capable. A triple threat to his composure. There were four more strongholds and several days hiking through varied ecosystems before this job was done. Somehow, he needed to get through it without revealing how much he admired Essian. Might be the most difficult thing he did, and as much as he felt they'd be able to converse more easily with each other, getting to know Essian better was only going to make this infatuation more awkward.

They'd been on the road for just under a month now, and were nearing the final stronghold on Essian's list. A couple of close calls from both Hilruda and wild animals, but it had been a surprisingly smooth journey, for which Essian thanked him regularly. Just one of many things that had changed over their close association. No sex, to the chagrin of his cock, but they'd grown more comfortable with each other. Took care of each other. Shared stories of growing up, compared life experiences.

There had been times Zerek had even seen Essian's humor. It was well hidden, but there, and Zerek loved getting that intimate glimpse of the man underneath the clan leader.

By mutual, unspoken consent, their conversation never veered to their recent history, the details of the true mate quest ceremonies, or anything sexual. Zerek didn't want to pressure Essian, and likely Essian didn't want to hurt Zerek with his disinterest. The fact that Essian seemed to care at all for his feelings was symptomatic of another problem.

It wasn't just his fascinating looks or the strong, visceral reaction his scent provoked. Essian exuded confidence, self-possession, and determination, all traits sorely lacking in most of the human men he came across. Hardly their fault—thanks to those pus gargling vampires—but it meant a man like Essian, human or not, entranced him. And over time, Zerek's feelings had deepened. The end of their quest was in sight. The last stronghold had become visible, this clan having built a large multi-story building. In an hour's time or less, they'd be at the gates. One day, maybe two, and then he'd be escorting Essian home, and he'd have to go back to a life that now seemed lacking.

"What about the other six clans? Don't you have to talk to them as well?" Surely Zerek could convince him they could talk to the interior clans together, whether it was about uniting the clans or trying to find homes where mistreated humans could settle.

"I spoke to them first. They aren't suffering incursions yet, but fortunately they were well aware of the issue."

"And they're willing to work with you?" Didn't take a genius to see that the border clans would be more likely to agree with Essian's plan.

"Grudgingly, but yes. There are a number of interpretations of that particular prophecy."

"What does your wife think of this plan? Interviewing people as though they have a chance at being your true mate." Zerek couldn't keep the snippishness out of his tone. It had been easy to put Essian's wife out of his mind while it was just the two of them, but soon, Essian would be returning to her, and Zerek hated her, just a bit, for that.

"My wife?"

"Your wife. Whoever is the mother of your children."

"None of them are my wife. Or my true mate."

Of course there was more than one. "Then how come so many children? Is that normal for your clan?"

"No. But this was a compromise I had with my father. As long as I secured heirs for the clan, he allowed me the freedom to seek a true mate rather than marry or bind with someone for dynastic reasons."

The lack of significant relationship in Essian's life shouldn't have any bearing on Zerek's moods, because he had no chance. However, hope was an insidious worm.

"What if you find your true mate on this quest of yours?" Zerek didn't want to think about it, but if a true mate was out there for Essian, it seemed likely he'd find her. Each stronghold filled Zerek with dread for that single reason.

"Then I will bind with whoever that is when the time is right. There are some who think the prophecy refers to a personal union for the leader of my clan."

Devious bastard, hedging his bets. Only made Zerek admire him even more. He was going to make a great warrior general when the time came.

CHAPTER SIX

Zerek flopped down on the bed, in a room that looked just like the others at all the other strongholds, although this was the most sumptuous so far. Someone besides the clan leader must know who Essian was. They'd arrived at the Tilia stronghold in the afternoon, and it was still early. Despite the long journey to get here, this was the first time Zerek had felt like his normal energetic self since being captured.

Bored. So fucking bored.

He'd been almost desperate to have some time to himself in the bathroom after Essian had been escorted away. Meant he had some time to pleasure himself while imagining Essian was there with him, touching him. The more time they spent together, the more often Essian let his tongue out to do whatever Kadrussian thing it did. He must have been demonstrating reserve in the early days, keeping the tongue inside his mouth. Only problem was that every appearance taunted Zerek, helpless to do anything but imagine what kind of oral skills Essian had.

His imagination had been quite vivid, but after each climax, an emptiness yawned inside him. He'd never know Essian's touch for real. He also tried to tell himself he'd get over this infatuation as soon as returned Essian to his clan territory, but he lied. His feelings ran deeper than infatuation and recovery would be longer than recuperating from a pit fight.

Zerek spent some time inspecting the walls for spy holes, but found none. They were either too well concealed or not all clans were as suspicious as Essian's people were. Then again, Essian was the one trying to change the way the clans dealt with each other. A dose of paranoia was probably healthy.

Fuck it. One of his major vices was curiosity, and if the boredom didn't kill him, wondering what sort of ceremony Essian was taking part in might. This would be his last chance to see it.

If there was a guard outside the suite, there was always the window. Perhaps there was no reason to guard him. After all, he was one measly human, and this clan had no reason to suspect Essian was here for any other purpose than to find a true mate.

The knob failed to turn in his hand, so Zerek tried again, hard enough that the door rattled, but didn't open. Just like the other strongholds, someone had fucking locked him in, with a giant platter of sumptuous foods.

He laughed without humor. Telling him he couldn't do something usually made him more determined to do just that. The Hilruda could vouch for that. Evil, soul-sucking garbage lovers. And now, he was feeling well enough that dinner and an orgasm wasn't going to make him pass out. If anyone managed to catch him—which they wouldn't—he hoped Essian's successful mission meant he'd be forgiving of such a minor transgression.

Zerek pulled out the handy lock pick pouch that was never far from his fingers and made short work of the lock.

Before he opened the door, he donned his hooded cloak, then stepped stealthily out into the hall. He didn't see or sense anyone nearby. Essian hadn't lied about the interest this quest thing generated. If Zerek didn't know better, he'd say the place was deserted.

Dusk approached, and shadows lengthened. Zerek took advantage of that and crept noiselessly in the dark, but for all the clanspeople he encountered, he could have danced through the halls.

It didn't take long to figure out where the crowd was; large gatherings of people made a distinct roar, even from a distance. The trick was to figure out a way to observe without being seen. Fortunately, Zerek had an almost preternatural skill for finding secrets.

Before night fell, he found his way into the rafters above a large open oval area covered by sand. At one end was a dais with a row of unoccupied chairs. The crowd of Kadrussians surrounding the sandy area had a collective air of anticipation, which meant Zerek hadn't missed the festivities.

They didn't wait long. Determining the age of Kadrussians wasn't easy unless they were very old or very young, but the men and women who stepped up onto the dais and filled the empty seats were likely the elder council, based on the fact that they were older than Essian, probably by twenty years or more. The noise of the crowd swelled and became thunderous when Essian and another Kadrussian appeared on the sand before the dais. Both men were shirtless. The stranger's coloration leaned to shades of blue and lavender with hints of gray or silver. He also was older than Essian.

The older man said something to the crowd, which, due to the acoustics of Zerek's position, he couldn't hear but the cheering crowd clearly could.

Zerek was going to assume this was Prosst, the Tilia clan leader, unless he was told otherwise.

Essian took up a position facing Prosst. They circled each other before lunging, grappling each other and falling to the sand.

Chills swept over Zerek's body, blood pounding in his ears. The two below him continued to fight while Zerek gripped the rafter harder and harder, knuckles whitening under the strain, until he could no longer feel his fingers. If he could, he'd have run away, but he was shaking so badly any additional movement would likely send him plunging to his death.

The remembered scent of blood filled his nose, as he recalled with sickening clarity the feel of flesh splitting under his fists.

Essian looked up, as though he'd heard someone call his name. Couldn't have been Zerek. If he were capable of making sounds, they wouldn't be as coherent as a name. The distraction cost Essian, but he recovered his ground quickly.

And still they fought—hard and vicious, although there was very little blood Zerek could see. The sound of the blows, though, made their way to his perch strangely magnified.

When Zerek thought he might pass out from this unexpected welter of emotions, Essian finally toppled his opponent to the ground and raised his arms in victory.

The crowd cheered, and Zerek concentrated on keeping his dinner in his belly. Prosst leapt to his feet and patted Essian on the back. A small bunch of young women, very well dressed, walked out on the sands, tongues flickering as they surrounded Essian.

Essian took one of the women's hand in his so her wrist faced up, then leaned over and licked her wrist. There was no mistaking the pleasure in her expression, and when Essian stopped, it was to take the wrist of another woman and perform the same procedure. The group of women pressed in closer, touching Essian's skin, and finally anger burned through Zerek's fear. He hadn't realized the memory of his pit fight and feeding of the Hilruda could be so devastating.

He used the anger to keep fear at bay as he escaped to the suite, his movements jerky and stiff. He paced around the room, fingers still trembling, as he decided whether or not he should just leave. He didn't think he could stay, though. The "ceremony" was too close to the pit fighting. Had Essian fed the crowd or had the crowd fed him? Or was it simply a way to boost the libido? Essian had locked him in a room while he went off and whored himself out for his cause, assuming he hadn't lied about that. Zerek was so desperate for revenge on the Hilruda, maybe he'd made himself an easy mark for Essian's lies.

A guttural shout ripped from his throat, and he swept the remaining food dishes to the floor. If he left, would they chase him?

He hadn't seen the locked door as a prison, not until he'd seen that fight. His situation hadn't improved, it had only been varnished to look pretty. Leave. He had to leave. His job was essentially over. Essian had said as much when they'd arrived at the final clan stronghold on the list. But the thought of leaving Essian behind, and never seeing him again was acutely painful. Then he realized it didn't matter. Whether he stayed or not, Essian didn't need him any longer. With shaking fingers, he gathered his things. Leaving during the distraction of the ceremony almost guaranteed he could leave unobserved.

The door burst open, and Essian, still half dressed, strode through. Zerek's knees wobbled and the tremors shaking his body got worse, but he stood his ground.

Essian wrapped his arms around him, and Zerek struggled until he realized Essian was attempting to soothe him. At the beginning of their journey, Essian wouldn't have tried such a thing, but they'd grown closer. Friends maybe. Or so Zerek had thought. A betrayal like this wasn't possible between friends.

"What's wrong?"

Zerek inhaled deeply, Essian's now familiar scent calming him. Not enough to let go of his concerns, but enough that he could at least function as a self-sufficient adult instead of a frightened child.

The embrace was all wrong. Essian had never touched him like this in the entire month they'd journeyed. Zerek would have given anything for it, but how could he accept it after what he'd seen?

He wormed out of Essian's arms. "Were you feeding?"

"What?" Their time together had improved Zerek's ability to read Essian's expressions, but he had a hard time believing Essian didn't know what he was talking about.

"Feed. I saw you fighting. The crowd. Do you take the same thing as the Hilruda?"

Essian's ears flattened against his head and his eyes widened. "You saw."

"That's not an answer, *Seeker*." Zerek spat the words.

"We're not like them. I promise you. I'd never hurt you like that. Many of us believe the Hilruda started the pit fights to mock our traditions."

Zerek wanted to believe, but he couldn't.

A frustrated snarl escaped Essian. "You're better. You've gotten stronger every day. Listen to your body. You are not diminished, are you?"

Unwillingly, he conceded Essian was right. In fact, he felt like an even better version of himself now that Essian had returned. That feeling of rightness would be a loss he'd have a hard time getting used to once Essian returned to his territory and the formidable task he'd set for himself.

"Then why were you doing it?" He only half meant the fighting.

Watching Essian lick someone other than him had been almost as horrifying.

"Come outside. The time for secrecy is almost over, but I wish to be able to speak freely."

Zerek nodded. He wanted answers and straight talk, not cryptic statements he had to pick apart to decipher meaning.

Essian busted the lock on the window, flipped it open and jumped outside. Zerek followed, and they walked away from the main house. The woods were too far away, but away from the windows, the night was dark, and despite the lack of vegetative cover, it seemed as though they were alone.

"The fight you saw, it's common in mate quests. It's the way to show a clan leader you're a worthy mate candidate for their relatives."

Jealousy burned through him. This true mate quest wasn't as much of a subterfuge as Essian would have him believe.

"How did this help with your negotiations?" Essian hadn't spoken of the ceremony in anything but the most vague terms, but there didn't seem to be any negotiation going on, aside from which woman was going to warm his bed first. Or which beds he'd warm, since Zerek had yet to deal with one of Essian's lovers in the set of rooms the clans assigned them.

"I told you, all the clan leaders would know me by sight. They all granted me a private audience, and the negotiations took place prior to the fight."

"Don't tell me that fight was just for show."

Essian rubbed at his shoulder. "No. Not at all. Prosst tried harder than he would have if I'd just been a Seeker. Because fighting is also how we show we're bargaining in good faith. It shows we have strength in our convictions, and have the strength to stand behind an agreement."

Never had Zerek been more aware he was trying to understand another species. And failing.

Essian wasn't finished. "It's also how we choose clan leaders. They have to prove themselves physically."

"But your daughter..." The Kadrussians didn't have a significant sexual difference related to size, but he would have hated to see a woman fighting that fight.

"My daughter will do well when the time comes. It's not about winning. It's about respect and holding your own. Proving yourself. Granted, I wouldn't have liked to have lost to Prosst, but I didn't need to win to gain his support."

Zerek rubbed his arms. It wasn't cold, but he was still jittery and didn't know what to do with his hands.

"And you promise there was no feeding." The concept still had the ability to make him feel sick. Probably always would.

"No. I'd never hurt you like that. Never. I wish you'd hadn't been forced to fight in the pit. We tried to get you out before your first fight, but the Hilruda acted too fast." Essian's tongue slipped out, but the movement seemed wary, tentative.

Today was the first day Zerek had completely shaken off the effects of the feeding in that pus riddled cesspool, which had to be the only reason he'd let Essian's attraction fog his normally sharp mental processes. It had taken three days to make the journey from Stony Gate to Essian's Serpentes stronghold. He'd been in Hilruda custody less than two days before his rescuers arrived.

Shock, cold and clarifying, swept through him and he came to standstill. Essian took a few steps before he turned to face Zerek.

"I'm so sorry you went through that. You'll never know how sorry." Essian's words were halting, as though he were unaccustomed to apologizing. Zerek was certain the apology was sincere, but Essian's remorse wasn't enough to wipe away the hurt.

"Which doesn't change the fact that you were behind my capture." It had to be true. There was no other way Essian's people could have gotten to him inside Stony Gate as quickly as they had.

Essian's mouth dropped open. "We...I needed your help."

"Let me guess. Gress works for you. Or is part of the Serpentes clan." The complete and utter betrayal was ripping his heart into shreds, and he swallowed heavily before he puked up every meal he'd ever eaten.

Essian reached for him, but Zerek ducked away. For the first time since they'd met, Zerek didn't want Essian to touch him.

"The plan was to ensure we'd know exactly where you'd be, so we could go in and get you."

"That doesn't make it any better, Seeker. You had contacts, resources. You could have hired me. Like everyone else does." Zerek had further deductions. "Let me guess. You wanted to show the Hilruda you could pull one over on them."

"I never expected...I was counselled...that gratitude for the rescue would buy your loyalty and cooperation more effectively than gold. If I could change things, I would. I swear on my father's grave."

Pain lanced through him at the callous and misguided manipulation of him.

"You... you..." His bottomless pool of epithets dried up, and without a verbal outlet for his pain, Zerek launched himself at Essian. The surprise allowed him to take the heavier man to the ground, breath exploding from him in a whoosh, but suddenly Zerek found himself in a grappling match much like the one he'd witnessed earlier.

With Essian's bigger size, keeping him down was a challenge, but Zerek managed it for a few moments while he got in a couple of punches to

Essian's chest. Essian flipped him over, and Zerek used the momentum to continue the roll. He pulled himself out of close quarters and leapt to his feet. Without surprise on his side, he wasn't big enough or strong enough to keep Essian on the ground.

Usually, he was the bigger one in a fight, and he used his bulk to his advantage. Now, he was going to have to take the opposite role, and hope he could hold his own. He ducked and evaded most of Essian's blows, but a couple glanced off him. They'd still bruise, but for some reason, Zerek didn't think they had as much power behind them as when he'd fought Prosst.

Good. A tired Essian might give him an advantage.

Zerek danced around Essian, striking when he found an opening, but Essian blocked well, and none of his blows found much substance. Essian didn't seem to be trying to hurt him, though, just control him and block his blows.

He put everything he had into it. All his anger, frustration, and jealousy, along with all his strength, but he was never able to best Essian. And after several minutes, he started wondering why he even wanted to. The worst of the betrayal had actually occurred before they'd even met. Callous, perhaps, but not a betrayal of the friendship they'd been building. Both of them were sweating and panting, Essian's spicy musk blooming around their tussle.

He had one last move, even though he knew it was doomed. Again, he launched himself at Essian, hoping the bigger man wouldn't have been expecting it.

He was right. Essian went down, winded, and Zerek pushed down on Essian's upper arms to pin him. But he'd worked out most of his anger, and after the pit fight, he wasn't ready to put anyone else down with his fists. Not if he could avoid it.

The unfettered access to Essian's body started having another effect, one that had his cock heavy and throbbing in his pants. He had to yield, get out of this close contact before Essian figured it out.

As he tried to extricate himself, his hand slipped on Essian's sweaty skin, and Zerek found himself flipped on the ground underneath Essian. He tried wrapping his arms around Essian to wrench him away, but Essian's muscles were like unyielding stone.

The self-satisfied grin on his face and the madly flickering tongue were too much. Zerek ground his hips upward, rubbing his erection against Essian and he nearly fainted when Essian growled and rubbed back with his own stiff cock.

Essian straddled him and clutched Zerek's shirt in both fists. He cocked his head to one side as though asking Zerek's permission. What else could he do but nod? Zerek wanted Essian, and was willing to forgive him. They'd have to talk after, but right now, Zerek wanted to fulfill a couple of fantasies.

Essian ripped his shirt away, then moved to remove their pants while Zerek squirmed in anticipation. Essian didn't disappoint. The tongue that featured in so many masturbatory sessions started at his lips and worked down, arousing Zerek more than he'd thought possible. Even the hint of fang occasionally scraping across his flesh didn't frighten him as it perhaps should have. Instead, he found himself leaning into the caresses, lust making him reckless.

When Essian finally got to his cock, that wild bifurcated tongue created a sensation no human could duplicate. Zerek's hips began thrusting helplessly as his orgasm barreled down on him.

All it took was Essian moving his fingers along Zerek's balls to delve between his cheeks, while keeping that tongue twining around his cock, and Zerek was done.

Zerek shouted, his muscles locked, and his cock fired pulse after pulse into Essian's welcoming mouth. Limp and sated, Zerek could only lay there while Essian threw his head back, letting out a hissing ululation of triumph, fangs fully extended. No one had ever looked sexier or more primal.

A still-erect cock nudged his leg, and Zerek wondered what the howl was for, it wasn't to signify Essian coming.

But then, Essian put his tongue back to work, and Zerek no longer cared. As though aware his cock was too sensitive for direct stimulation this soon, Essian focused on extremities. Zerek had never had his feet or ankles licked or kissed, but he'd been missing out. A small flash of jealousy reared its head when Essian sucked on the inside of his wrists, knowing each candidate for his quest had enjoyed this same sensation.

When Essian moved to the inside of his elbows, though, Zerek's jealousy disappeared as his cock rose valiantly to the stimulation, far quicker than he'd expected. Instead of moving in on Zerek's cock, Essian leaned to the side, holding up a tiny pot.

Breathless with desire, Zerek still had to ask. "What is that?" Surely Essian hadn't planned to fuck him.

Sheepish was another expression that rarely graced Essian's beautiful face. "Lubrication. The clan leader usually provides it, whether it'll be used or not. It was in my pocket."

Irritation tamped down some of Zerek's arousal. "Was Prosst expecting you to find your true mate? How would you know, anyway?"

Essian stroked his chest gently, and without urgency, even though his erection thrust rampantly from his body.

"There are several clues, but tasting is the definitive proof."

Son of a farting donkey. Essian had been tasting all those women as a true mate test. His jealousy hadn't been unfounded, which didn't ease his mind any, or explain the lubrication.

"As for expectations...if there is doubt, a more intimate taste is required. Whether one finds a true mate or not, people are aroused, sex often occurs, and since a candidate can be male or female...lubrication is provided."

Zerek levered himself up on his elbows. "You mean every time you left me alone in the room to go to those fucking true mate gatherings, you were fucking your brains out with whatever woman crossed your path?"

Essian stroked his chest more firmly. "Calm down. I participated in the tasting, to convince any observers that I was a simple Seeker, but sex is not required as part of the ceremony, nor did I indulge."

Truth rang in Essian's words, dispelling Zerek's ire. Not that he could have fought against the pleasure of Essian plucking at his nipples and tracing the trail of hair on his belly. As though trying to draw Essian's attention, his cock twitched.

Moving back so he could settle between Zerek's legs, Essian then opened the jar and scooped out a glistening glob.

Zerek spread his legs in silent invitation, his cock a heated log lying heavy against his hip. While Essian slicked and stretched him, his tongue stayed busy, but this time swirling around his balls. All too soon, Zerek was ready to blow again, amazed Essian had held out as long as he had.

When Essian lifted his head and nudged his hips, Zerek flipped over onto his hands and knees with alacrity. The sensation of someone bigger than him mounting him from behind was unusual, but welcome. Essian's scent got stronger, and oddly, there wasn't even a twinge of pain when Essian pushed his impressive cock into Zerek's body. Nevertheless, Essian held his hips still, while that mobile miracle of a tongue danced along Zerek's spine, making him shiver.

"Move already," Zerek demanded.

Essian obeyed, even though there probably weren't many people who dared command him. The slow slide of cock in and out quickly sped up, Zerek moving his hips back to meet Essian's thrusts, both of them chasing climax together.

The power behind Essian's thrusts meant Zerek couldn't move a hand to get a grip on his cock, but it didn't matter. With every stroke, Essian's thick cock massaged his prostate and he wasn't going to need a hand to get off.

Suddenly, he became aware of eyes on them. Zerek turned his head slightly, only to see several Kadrussians watching. The only one he recognized was Prosst.

Zerek was too far gone to care that they had an audience. Maybe it even made him more desperate for the climax Essian could give him.

"Harder." This time, the command came out more as a breathless squeal, but Essian obeyed again.

Behind him, Essian let out another triumphant bellow, cock pulsing inside him. Fangs bit into his shoulder, and the sudden wash of pain exploded into orgasm. Breath stuttering, Zerek's cock striped the grass below him. He had a moment to realize that those fangs had probably poisoned him, but he was too sated to care. His arms slid out, no longer able to support his weight, and darkness took him.

CHAPTER SEVEN

When Zerek awoke, it was full daylight. He stretched, feeling a little foggy. For some reason, Essian slept slumped in a chair beside his bed, his beautiful copper and bronze skin looking strangely ashy.

"Hey." Zerek reached out a hand to prod Essian. What was Essian doing in here anyway? As usual, they'd been assigned a suite with separate bedrooms. At least, he thought so. He didn't remember this room at all.

Another man—Prosst—entered the room as Essian bolted upright. He wasn't sure what Prosst was doing in the bedroom, nor why the man made him wary, but Essian looked worried.

No, that wasn't right. Essian did look worried, but the weight of that worry sat around Zerek's neck, which was odd. There was no reason for Essian to worry, nor was there any reason for Zerek to take that same worry on his own shoulders.

"How are you feeling?" Essian stroked his arm, and that weird worry eased, like taking off an uncomfortable shirt.

"Fine. Good." Except he couldn't feel any of the ghostly physical reminders of sex, so that had to have been a particularly vivid erotic dream. Shame. "What's going on?"

"You've been unconscious for almost two days."

Two days, that couldn't be right. He didn't feel sick. Sitting up, he did a quick mental assessment, but he merely felt rested. No, he felt better than rested. He was energized and alert. He might even go so far as to say amazing. Except he couldn't remember how he ended up in bed. He had no sense of those missing days.

Prosst strode over to the bed and loomed over him, staring at him for a moment before he turned back to Essian. "I'll act as witness, if needed. We'll talk soon."

"Thank you." Essian clasped his shoulder, then Prosst left.

57

"Witness?"

Essian's skin tone improved as Zerek watched. Had Essian been ill, too? Instead of answering, Essian responded with another question. "May I get in with you?"

His memory was still disjointed, but he was starting to think the sex hadn't been a dream. Either way, he wasn't about to deny Essian, not when he had the nagging feeling that Essian belonged there.

Essian slid in beside him and wrapped an arm around him. Zerek wasn't going to complain, especially as they were both shirtless, and he cuddled into the Essian's chest. Touching made the world seem better; he'd be a fool to pass that up.

"Do you remember anything? From two nights ago?"

Zerek sighed. "Give me a minute." His fingers moved lightly over Essian's skin as he tried to remember.

Before the bits and pieces coalesced, Essian spoke. "I bit you."

"You bit me." Self-loathing and pride swirled around his ears, and he wasn't sure why he'd be feeling either of those things. But the reminder coaxed him fully awake. "Did you poison me? You weren't...trying to kill me, were you?"

Essian's hiss was disappointed. "No. Not at all." He stroked Zerek's back, and the only feelings that remained were love, inside and out of Zerek's head. Falling in love with Essian was probably the stupidest thing he'd ever done, but for now, Zerek was going to revel in what he had. It was more than he'd ever expected.

"Then what?"

"There's never been record of a human true mate before. Probably because our bites are dangerous, if not lethal, to humans."

"You bite to bond a true mate?" Zerek's hand reached up to clasp his neck where Essian had bit him. Not even a scab remained.

"Yes." Essian kissed his forehead. "And you are mine."

"But I can't be your true mate. How is that possible?"

"The signs were there. The first time I caught your scent, I realized it was possible. But I was scared. If I was wrong, I could kill you. I nearly did."

Guilt nearly suffocated him, which didn't make sense, so he made an effort to push it away. Probably some side effect of the venom.

"What other signs?"

Essian tucked him closer. "This. Being near me soothed you. Calmed you, even as I excited you."

"You knew?" How humiliating. But he had to admit the truth. Every time he was close to Essian, he felt better.

"Yes. It was the same for me."

Oh. That was far less humiliating. "So, you decided to bite me to test your theory?"

"No, of course not. Do you remember me telling you taste told us the truth?"

Zerek's cock plumped up as those memories returned with full erotic force. "Uh, yes." His voice had thickened. "You know, I'd have been up for a taste test any time during the last month."

Essian groaned. "One of the reasons for fighting before a candidate search is that the fight releases pheromones. My pheromones help intensify the taste, help us to avoid making a mistake. When you attacked me, you triggered my pheromones, which in turn triggered yours. I was drowning in a scent that screamed of true mate, and I had to taste. One touch of my tongue to your skin, and I knew, but I was still afraid of making a mistake."

"Oh. A more intimate taste was required." Zerek had thought he'd long ago lost the ability to blush, but he'd been wrong. The howl of triumph after he'd come in Essian's mouth made more sense, even if he was completely the wrong choice.

"Then, inside your body, I couldn't stop myself from giving you the bonding bite, even though..." Essian turned his face away. "Even though there are still things I haven't told you."

There were a number of things that needed to be addressed, so Zerek had to decide which to choose first.

"How do you know the bonding bite even took?" Essian obviously believed in the true mate thing, but he hadn't told Zerek anything that couldn't be chalked up to pheromones working overtime.

"A real bonding allows us to sense the emotions of our true mate. Which is why a bond gone wrong is a perversion of something sacred. None of those shared emotions will be happy or comforting. Being close to each other is like being stung by insects, rather than soothing."

Pushing against Essian's chest, Zerek raised himself up to stare down at Essian. "You meant these emotions that seem like they're outside my head are yours?"

That might be the most unbelievable thing he'd heard yet, but there was no mistaking the tender look Essian gave him, nor could he explain the buffeting sensation of love, like being stroked with butter soft leather.

Another memory came back to him. "Didn't you say that true mates were equals? We're so far from equals it's not even funny. You're a clan leader and I'm a smuggler."

Essian laughed. "Equals in the relationship, not necessarily equals in life station. You've never once treated me as a superior, nor have you let me treat you as though you didn't deserve equal treatment. You don't know how much I treasure that; it's one of the rewards of a true mate."

Zerek wanted to snort, but he had been adamant about not letting anyone, not even Essian, intimidate him. That didn't mean they were true mates, though. How could it?

"I can sense your disbelief, but there is one other sign of a true bond." Essian grabbed a small hand mirror from the table next to the bed and handed it to him. "Look at your neck."

Zerek shifted to catch the light on his neck. He knew without asking Essian meant the side he'd bitten. A patch of skin was discolored. Except that it matched the mottled bronze and copper of Essian's skin perfectly. Zerek rubbed at it, then licked a finger and rubbed some more, but the color didn't smudge or budge, but merely tingled.

"This is proof your body assimilated and accepted me. My venom will no longer be a danger to you."

Zerek narrowed his eyes suspiciously. "Does this mean you intend to bite me again?" He wasn't sure if he was more scared or turned on by the prospect.

"Come here." Essian didn't wait for him to comply, but instead slid around him sinuously, and rubbed a fang over the patch. The arousal that had been on a low simmer since Essian had gotten into bed with him boiled over, sending blood rushing to his cock.

Essian kissed his cheek. "I'm sorry. I only meant to prove a point."

Point proved. Zerek didn't have much choice but to be convinced of the existence of true mates. They still had more to discuss, and Zerek willed his cock to relax, because he didn't think he'd be happy about the conversation to come.

"What else are you hiding?" The guilt was there, under the warm and rosy feelings, now that he was paying attention. If Essian had claimed him earlier, it was possible those loving feelings wouldn't have been there yet to compensate for the stuff Zerek was going to hate. As it was, Zerek didn't think there was much he couldn't forgive, especially now that he'd know if Essian lied. That would be his true mate reward—someone he could trust unequivocally.

"I had always intended to ask you to fight me. As a negotiation. As I did with the other clan leaders."

Again, Zerek was lost in cross-cultural confusion. "Before we even met? Surely the pheromone thing wouldn't have worked if we weren't true mates. What were you hoping to get out of it?"

"You asked me once if the united clans had enough people to go against the Hilruda. The answer is no. We don't. We need to unite with the humans. It's the only way." Essian was convinced he spoke the truth.

"Why me? I'm just a smuggler."

"No. Not just a smuggler. They tell stories about you. Your exploits are well known and you give humans hope for a better life. You're the closest to a human clan leader your people have, and I always intended to come to terms with you. Between your true mate status and Prosst witnessing the fight, the rest of my people will accept you as an honorary clan leader."

"That's what Prosst said he'd witness? The fight? But I didn't win."

Essian flicked his tongue against Zerek's cheek, and Zerek sensed it was an intimacy reserved for lovers and mates.

"You don't need to win, remember? You just need to hold your own, and you did more than that. You impressed both me and Prosst with your determination and stamina. Even before today, I had come to treasure our relationship, and admire your courage, resourcefulness, and conviction."

His reservations were melting under Essian's pride in him, and the thought of throwing off the Hilruda oppressors' yoke was more important than any other objections he had. "Clan leader. I don't think I'm right for the job, but I'll take it for now. There is one thing I don't understand, though. Humans have been on your planet for a relatively short time. How did the Hilruda survive before? How come my ancestors didn't realize they needed that much energy? Did they sacrifice their own people before the Bitter Silence?"

Essian laughed bitterly. "Sometimes, but it's mostly a case of greed. They don't need anywhere near as much energy as they take, but you humans are so...volatile. They've been salivating for their chance since your people landed. After so many years, they're intoxicated. Addicted. And there's only one outcome."

"Annihilation."

Essian nodded. "Annihilation. Ours or theirs."

"Then let's get back home and start planning our war."

Essian's pleasure in his words was almost like a caress. Home. He hadn't had a home since his grandfather had died, but there was one waiting in the Serpentes stronghold.

"One last thing, Seeker." This time, his emphasis wasn't sneering, but affectionate.

"No. I am Seeker no longer. The quest is done." Essian flicked his tongue over Zerek's neck.

"You never told me, what was the prophecy exactly?"

"When threefold becomes twofold, seek salvation from the stars above and the ground below. Find redemption in the union of the snake."

"That's it? That's all you had to go on?" Would have taken more faith than Zerek had. "How did you develop a plan from two lines that don't even mention humans at all?"

Essian hissed joyfully. "I studied more than other Kadrussians, because I was so rarely allowed play time or excursions. The seers fascinated me, and I studied their teachings extensively. The concept of threefold refers to humans settling on our planet. But now, we're no longer three equal species, so we've become twofold again. And the humans came to us from the stars, so that part was clear to me."

"And the ground below?"

"I found you in the ground below Stony Gate."

How very literal. "Well, at least I can see why you weren't sure if you were supposed to find a mate or unite the clans."

Essian's expression became quite smug. "Or both."

Zerek laughed. "Or both. Wily snake."

Essian nodded, but there was still one thing Zerek had to say on the matter.

"When we get back, we need to deal with whoever suggested you follow that ridiculous plan to turn me over to the Hilruda. You realize they were trying to sabotage your plan, right? They didn't want you to fulfill the prophecy." If it weren't for the unexpected true mate thing, and there was no reason for anyone to anticipate such a thing, Zerek would never have given Essian a chance to explain. He certainly wouldn't have trusted him enough to unite their clans—all of them—against the Hilruda.

"I know." The bitter pain of betrayal was familiar, but the emotion belonged to Essian. "Before we go back and clean house, let me show you how much I love you."

"I love you too." Zerek let Essian coax him onto his back. The enormous task Essian had set himself was now also Zerek's responsibility, and would be part of their lives for years to come. He wasn't about to miss out on the chance for pleasure with his true mate whenever the opportunity presented itself.

He opened up his arms and his heart to the man he'd never thought he'd have.

THE END

ABOUT THE AUTHOR

KC Burn has been writing for as long as she can remember and is a sucker for happy endings (of all kinds). After moving from Toronto to Florida for her husband to take a dream job, she discovered a love of gay romance and fulfilled a dream of her own -- getting published. After a few years of editing web content by day, and neglecting her supportive, understanding hubby and needy cat at night to write stories about men loving men, she was uprooted yet again and now resides in California. Writing is always fun and rewarding, but writing about her guys is the most fun she's had in a long time, and she hopes you'll enjoy them as much as she does.

www.ingramcontent.com/pod-product-compliance
Lightning Source LLC
Chambersburg PA
CBHW020647130626
46552CB00003B/1439